C000002543

PETER J MURRAY

POPPY WARRIOR

PETER J MURRAY

POPPY WARRIOR

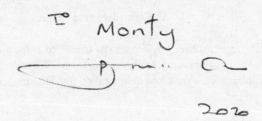

To Monty

2020

ATLANTIS CHILDREN'S BOOKS

Copyright © 2019 Peter J. Murray
Cover illustration © 2019 Paul Bryn Davies
Chapter illustrations © 2019 Simon Murray

Author photograph © 2019 Andy Muscroft

Graphic Design & Typesetting © 2019 Louise Drew
www.rivercastlegraphics.co.uk

First published in Great Britain in 2019
by Atlantis Children's Books

www.atlantischildrensbooks.com

ISBN-13: 978-0-9571088-9-9

All Rights Reserved.

The right of Peter J. Murray to be identified as the author
of this work has been asserted by him in
accordance with the Copyright Designs and Patents Act 1988.

A CIP catalogue record for this book is available from
the British Library.

Printed and bound by CPI Group(UK) Ltd, Croydon, CR0 4YY

This book is dedicated to our good friend, Julie Davies, who passed after a long battle with illness in August, 2018.

There is a poignant parallel between Julie and the countless men who gave their lives during the Great War of 1914-18...neither complained of their suffering, but faced their battles with incredible bravery.

...And they will never be forgotten because they are truly inspiring to all of us that follow.

PJM

PETER J MURRAY

POPPY WARRIOR

ATLANTIS CHILDREN'S BOOKS

PROLOGUE

Beneath a cold grey moon the poppies glow.

Amid the blood-red blooms, a ghostly sombre soldier stands with head hung low.

His quest — the mortal boy to find

Unite the past and present within the swirling mists of space and time.

Our long dead phantom will once more draw breath

To show his naive charge the bloodied battlefields of death.

They'll walk beyond the hellish trenches, cross the land of tangled wire and muddied clod

To see an unsung hero's selfless act of gallantry, played out before the ever-watching eyes of God.

And now to stand amid the endless lines of crosses, to show his bloodline son

The massive loss of life...the cruel cost of how this futile war was won.

Alas, the countless corpses now at peace sit in lines upon their heavenly pews

And each of us should pray for them...**remember them**

And pray that God remembers, too!

PJM

NEW SCHOOL

Prepare to turn right.

Jess Palmer laughed as her mother nodded towards the dashboard. 'It's not a real person, Mum. It's only a Satnav.'

Josh managed a faint smirk but didn't bother to look up. He was far too busy concentrating on the iPad.

In two hundred metres, turn right.

'Almost there,' Mrs Palmer said enthusiastically. She glanced at the digital clock on the facia. '...And ten minutes early. Great!'

As the white hatchback made a turn, Jess leaned forward from her place in the back seat and stared through the windscreen towards the closed school gates. 'I'll get out and tell them we're here.'

Josh remained fixed on the iPad. Mrs Palmer slowed

11

the car to a stop and Jess stepped out. She made her way over to the intercom by the school gate, pushed the button and waited for a response.

Mrs Palmer turned to her son in the passenger seat. 'Aren't you excited about your new school, Josh? You've not even looked up! What's so interesting on the iPad?'

'Front Line 1,' Josh muttered, his fingers going crazy over the keypad. 'Nearly reached the enemy machine-gun post. Killed at least 20 Germans so far. Just need a few more minutes...'

Mrs Palmer shook her head and sighed.

As Jess slipped back into the car and the school gates opened, Mrs Palmer drove the car through slowly and entered the car park.

Jess gasped. 'Mum! Look! They're amazing! Blood red!'

At the mention of 'blood', Josh looked up for the first time.

'I've never seen such a show of poppies in all my life,' Mrs Palmer agreed, gazing over to her left.

'So many,' Jess added excitedly.

As much as Josh wasn't into flowers, he had to agree... *inside his head, at least!*

Safely parked, Mrs Palmer and the twins got out and stood by the rear of the car. They stared over at the mass of poppies growing along the embankment between the edge of the car park and the school railings.

'Maybe the pupils planted them,' Mrs Palmer said admiringly.

Jess nodded. 'There must be thousands.'

'Millions!' Josh chipped in.

Mrs Palmer focused their attention. 'Come on, you

two!' she said sternly. 'Let's remember why we're here. The Head will be expecting us in a few minutes. We'd better get inside.'

Josh sensed his twin sister's slight nervousness as she grabbed Mum's hand. He joined them as they stared towards the sign by the double glass doors.

PHEASANT BANK ACADEMY
SCHOOL RECEPTION

As the three of them set off towards the school building, Josh couldn't resist glancing over his shoulder at the mass of crimson flowers stretching back towards the school gates...*and wondering why the sight of them was sending shivers down his spine.*

*

The bell for the mid-morning break rang out as the Palmers walked through the school entrance into the reception area. A moment later a wave of children swept by, chatting and laughing loudly. Josh stared at the sea of faces...but no one looked back.

Why should they? They all knew each other...but no one knew him!

He began to feel a twinge of nervousness in the pit of his stomach.

A loud voice called out from somewhere in front, 'HELLO...THIS WAY. WE'LL SIGN YOU IN LATER WHEN THE RUSH HAS DIED DOWN.'

Josh looked up and saw the smiling face of a lady beckoning them towards her.

'MAKE WAY, CHILDREN! REMEMBER YOUR

MANNERS. LET OUR GUESTS THROUGH.'

The tide of children stopped abruptly, making enough room for the three visitors to pass through the reception area into a small corridor.

'You must be the Palmers,' the kind lady smiled again. 'I'm the head teacher, Miss Robinson. Please come this way. We'll go into my office. Much quieter in there!'

A short while later, Josh and his sister were seated either side of their mother, facing their new head teacher on the other side of a large oak desk. The receptionist had signed them into the visitors' book and Miss Robinson had ordered tea and squash.

She spoke proudly to her three guests about the ethos of the school. 'We're a very caring school,' she said. 'Everyone is treated as an equal and we believe in bringing out the best in each and every individual.'

'Speaking of 'best',' Mrs Palmer said, 'that show of poppies out there is the *best* I've ever seen. Did the school plant them?'

Miss Robinson shook her head. 'No one knows who planted them. They've been with us for as long as anyone can remember. We're very proud of them; they serve to remind staff and children of those who gave their lives for us during the war. It's a subject we often touch on... especially in our History lessons.'

'Brilliant!' Josh found himself blurting out. 'The war was amazing!'

'Not the words I would choose to describe it,' Miss Robinson smiled.

Mrs Palmer frowned.

Jess leaned forward in her seat. 'Inappropriate

adjective!'

The head teacher looked impressed. She turned to Mrs Palmer. 'I see by their latest school reports that both twins are bright, to say the least.'

'Too bright by half, sometimes,' Mrs Palmer sighed.

Miss Robinson looked from one twin to the other. 'Would you mind being in the same class?' She glanced at Mrs Palmer. 'We're a three-form entry so we *could* put them into different classes.'

'No point,' Josh said matter-of-factly. 'Same class or different class – we always know what each of us is up to and what we're thinking.'

'It's true,' Mrs Palmer nodded. 'They can just about read each other's minds. Barring gender, they're identical in more ways than you think!'

Josh noted that Miss Robinson was now looking at them curiously. 'That's settled then,' she said firmly. 'You'll both be in Viking Class and we'll look forward to seeing the two of you on Monday morning. Do you have any questions?'

After a few routine questions, mainly from Mrs Palmer, and a few routine answers from Miss Robinson, everyone agreed they were about finished.

Josh sniffed the air. 'Just one final question. Can I ask what that strange smell is...sort of sweet and smoky?'

'Pipe tobacco,' Jess answered.

'Can you smell it?' Josh asked his sister.

She shook her head. 'No. But if it's sweet and smoky, that's what it *must* be.'

'I can't smell anything,' Mrs Palmer said.

'Me neither,' the head teacher added. 'But years ago,

this school was commissioned as an administrative centre during the war and no doubt many of the men who worked here smoked pipes. It's a curious thing, but a few other staff have said they've detected the smell of tobacco from time to time.'

Jess stared over at her twin brother and tweaked her nose. 'Especially those with a super-strong sense of smell,' she laughed.

'Or those who can tune into a ghostly energy trapped in a building...' Josh said in a spooky voice.

Miss Robinson forced a smile and quickly changed the subject. 'Well if that's all, I'll see you back to reception. It's been a pleasure meeting you, and I look forward to monitoring the progress of your delightful twins, Mrs Palmer.'

'Good luck with that!' Mrs Palmer said jokingly.

They thanked the head teacher and made their way back towards the reception area. The twins walked close behind their mother and Josh glowered at his sister as she tweaked her nose again and giggled.

...She was reading his mind again and she knew that he was still thinking about that strange smell in the head teacher's office.

NEW TOWN

Rossfield looked interesting. It had a huge church at the start of a long straight High Street with lots of shops, cafés and restaurants. There was also a picturesque canal running by the edge of the town, with a line of colourful canal barges moored along its neat gravel towpath.

This place had a very different feel to the village they'd left behind on the outskirts of Manchester. Though not far from the city, the hills of the Peak District had loomed over their little community and had given them a feeling of protection. It was a place where everyone knew everyone.

But Josh was glad that Dad had got a promotion in his job as a heating engineer and moved them to this bigger place. Of course, he and Jess had been sad to leave their friends behind, but they were equally excited about the adventure that lay ahead.

Josh found himself standing by his twin sister, staring into the window of one of Rossfield's many charity shops. He caught sight of his reflection...straw blonde hair and striking blue eyes. If his hair had been three inches longer and down to his collar, he might just as well have been staring at Jess!

But it was something beyond his reflection that really caught his attention....a soldier's helmet...*and it looked real!*

'Can we go inside, Mum? I'd like to have a look around.'

Mrs Palmer nodded. 'Yes. I wouldn't mind having a browse myself.'

Once inside, Josh made a beeline for the helmet. Jess followed him. Mrs Palmer was quickly preoccupied, scanning through the clothes racks.

Josh picked up the steel helmet. It felt strangely warm.

Jess took it off him and examined it. 'It feels so cold,' she said.

Josh took it back. It still felt warm to him. He examined it more closely. The surface of the helmet was a dark green-brown colour, smooth, but with a small round dent in it. The helmet had a leather chin strap which hung loosely and looked well worn. He placed the helmet on his head. It was far too big and tilted clumsily to one side.

Jess laughed loudly. 'I won't tell you what you look like!'

Mrs Palmer joined them; she was carrying a brightly-coloured top on a hanger. 'What are you two up to?'

It was Jess who replied. 'Josh thinks he looks cool in that war helmet. But he looks like a dork!'

Josh removed the helmet from his head and held it tightly to his chest. 'Can I buy it, Mum?'

'You mean, can *I* buy it?' Mrs Palmer sighed. 'How much is it?'

Josh examined it again but couldn't find a price tag. He shook his head. 'Shall I ask someone?'

An elderly lady with a beaming smile walked up to them. 'Can I help?'

Mrs Palmer smiled back at her. 'We were just wondering how much this old war helmet is.'

The lady looked puzzled. 'Well…I've really no idea. We don't usually sell war artefacts. I'll just ask my colleague.'

The lady returned with a smartly-dressed younger man. He frowned when he saw Josh holding the helmet. 'That's odd!' he exclaimed. 'Where on earth did that come from?' He gestured to Josh to pass him the helmet. 'I don't know anything about this…a relic from the Second World War, no doubt. It's heavy, isn't it?'

'World War One, actually,' Josh corrected him. 'It's a British MK1 Brodie Helmet. It weighs about two and half pounds and it's made of steel. You can see where the iron in this small round dent has rusted. The leather strap isn't flexible and it has a nickel buckle. Some of the soldiers broke their necks on the straps when a bomb blast made them jolt their necks back, and that's why Second World War helmets have a flexible strap.'

Josh looked up and saw that his mum, Jess and the man were staring at him open-mouthed.

'Well…if you'd like to make a small donation, your son is welcome to it,' the man said to Mrs Palmer. 'He certainly knows his stuff!'

19

Mrs Palmer walked with the man over to the pay desk and left Josh and Jess staring at the helmet.

'How come you knew all that stuff?' Jess asked her brother.

Josh stared back at her with big eyes. 'I've no idea. That 'stuff', as you call it, came into my head just like someone was telling it to me. It's so weird.'

'You *are* weird,' Jess laughed. 'Always were and always will be.' She snatched the helmet, put it on her head and ran over to her mum at the pay desk.

Josh would normally have chased after her and snatched it back again. But this time he stood rooted to the spot...*deep in thought!*

*

Saturday night, and Jess was watching TV with Mum and Dad; Josh was up in his 'new' bedroom, playing Front Line 1 on his computer. He'd almost reached the enemy machine-gun post again, men from his regiment falling beside him, victims of the streams of German bullets. Adrenalin pulsed through Josh's veins as he fired back continuously, taking out snipers firing from the top of the enemy trench in front of him.

'Yes...yes...yes...' he said to himself through clenched teeth as his virtual rifle took out one virtual sniper after another.

He pushed on through the battlefield, dodging the deadly hail of bullets coming from the machine-gun post. *Nearly there...now's the time to use the grenade.*

He watched the monitor with bated breath as his

avatar threw itself to the ground and hurled a small object towards the machine gun post on top of the enemy trench. With deadly accuracy, it struck the target.

BOOM!!

Realistic screams. Realistic thick black smoke engulfing the enemy gun post. Realistic success for Josh.

'YESSSSSS!'

His fingers moved over the keyboard, bringing the mini-icon of himself back to its feet. Charging forward again and joined by a line of men advancing from behind, he reached the enemy trench, shooting dead any of the enemy's soldiers that tried to climb out.

BZZZZZZZZ....PHUT!

The screen turned black as the computer lost power.

I don't believe this, Josh thought to himself. *The first time I've reached Level 3 and it's crashed!*

Before Josh had time to do anything, the computer regained power and the screen burst back to life. Josh leaned forward and peered at the strange image that had replaced the interactive war game.

A woman wearing all black was standing with her back to the camera, in front of a big ornamental cross. He noticed the shops over her shoulder and saw that the bottom of the cross was covered in red flowers, most of them arranged in circular wreaths. Josh recognised them at once as poppies. As he continued to stare at the screen, the camera zoomed in on the marble cross; it had writing engraved on it. The camera zoomed closer still and Josh saw that it was a list of names, one on top of the other and seemingly in alphabetical order. The camera moved ever closer until Josh was able to read the names:

LAWRENCE MATTHEWS
CHARLES MORRISON
JOHN PHILIP NEIL

Josh realised he was looking at a war memorial. He had no idea why, or what was happening, but he somehow got the feeling that it was all for his benefit. The camera panned slowly downwards...

MARK NOBLE
GEORGE ALFRED ORMKIRK
STANLEY OSWALD PALMER...

The camera stopped its downward movement and zoomed in further:

STANLEY OSWALD PALMER

As Josh watched, fascinated, the camera drew back behind the lady in black, still standing in front of the cross. Josh had forgotten about her. She turned to face the camera as it closed in on her veiled face.

Josh swallowed hard as she slowly lifted her veil. At first, she just looked like an elderly woman, aged but pretty. But as the camera focused on her wrinkled face, Josh saw the tears trickling down her pale cheeks and sensed the immense grief in her sad staring eyes.

He decided he didn't want to see any more. He moved the cursor with the mouse to switch off the monitor...*but it wouldn't switch off.*

He reached down to the plug socket at the side of his desk and flicked the OFF switch. He knew well that this was bad practice, but he was desperate to cut the power and reboot the computer back to normal.

He looked back to the screen.

The lady was still there, her intense eyes cutting into

him. 'Come to the memorial, Josh, and say a prayer for my husband.'

Her voice sounded loud and clear. Josh pinched himself. He couldn't believe this was happening.

PHHHUUUT!

The screen turned black. The monitor had finally turned off.

A moment later, Josh found himself walking slowly downstairs. As if in a trance, he walked into the sitting room and sat down in silence, staring with unseeing eyes at the TV.

'Good of you to join us,' his mum said. 'Have you finally managed to win the war?'

Josh didn't answer. He stared blankly into space, wondering what had just happened...*and sensing strongly that this was only the beginning.*

SETTLING IN

It was Sunday night and Josh was in his bedroom getting a few things ready for Monday morning. Tomorrow would be his and Jess's first day at their new school and Mum was determined that they would make a good start. She'd given them both a very neatly written list of what to put in their school bags and Josh had just got around to packing his PE kit when a familiar knock sounded on his bedroom door.

KNOCK…KNOCK, KNOCK.

One knock, a pause, and then two quicker knocks; this was the code the twins used to signal their presence. Any other kind of knocking was probably parental…often to be ignored! As far as Josh and Jess were concerned, their bedrooms were 'adult-free zones'.

'OK,' Josh called out. 'You can come in.'

Jess strolled in, leapt into the air and landed on her back on Josh's bed. He was sitting at his desk staring at his computer, completely baffled that it was all working normally again.

'So what's going on exactly?' Jess asked, staring up at the ceiling with her hands behind her head.

'What do you mean?'

'Hmmm. Where do I start?' She turned to face him. 'First...there was that business in the charity shop. All that stuff you knew about the war helmet. Did it really just come into your head?'

Josh stood up from his desk, walked over to a shelf and took down the helmet. 'I'm not making it up. I promise, I never read it anywhere. It was as if somebody was filling up my brain with all that info. It really freaked me out!'

He walked over to his sister and sat on the end of the bed. 'And take a look at this.' He held out the helmet and turned it upside down. Jess sat up and looked to where Josh was pointing. She saw the faded letters written on one side of the fabric lining:

S.O.P.

'Hmmm. Maybe the owner of the helmet?'

Josh nodded. 'Possibly.'

'And there's another thing...' Jess said, stretching back on the bed. '...Just recently you've been very quiet. And it's not just me that's noticed. Mum and Dad have been on about it too. I overheard them. Dad says it's down to the move. He thinks you're maybe getting a bit edgy about things.'

'And what does Mum think?'

'She agrees. She says some people cope with change

25

better than others.'

'Like you, I suppose,' Josh sighed, going back over to his desk.

'So why *are* you acting so quiet?' Jess asked him. 'It's not *all* down to that helmet, surely.'

Josh sat down at his desk and turned to face his sister. He explained to her in vivid detail what had happened on his computer.

Jess sat up again and stared at her brother with big eyes, 'Wow! Now you're starting to freak *me* out.'

'Do you believe in a sixth sense?' Josh asked her.

'Course,' Jess replied. 'I always get a funny feeling when something good or bad is going to happen. To be honest, I had a feeling you were going to tell me about something spooky as soon as I knocked on the door.'

Josh stared at his sister with a serious expression. 'Well, I've got a strong feeling that these weird things are only the beginning.'

'So what are you going to do?' Jess asked.

'Well for a start, *we* are going to find the war memorial where that woman was standing.'

'The woman with the black veil and the creepy eyes?'

Josh nodded.

'But how?'

'That war memorial...it was close to a shop...*Warners Dry Cleaners*.'

Jess swung her legs round and sat upright. 'Never heard of it.'

'Maybe it's in Rossfield. We could ask around at school tomorrow,' Josh suggested.

'Worth a try,' Jess replied, rising to her feet and

yawning at the same time. 'See you in the morning. Sleep tight.'

'You, too!' Josh called after her.

But inwardly, Josh knew he would *not* get a good night's sleep. Far too much to think about, and as he'd just said to his sister...*he felt sure that this was only the very beginning!*

*

Josh did *not* sleep easily that night. He tossed and turned and began dreaming...a dream that quickly turned into a nightmare.

He was charging through a battlefield, just like the one in his Front Line 1 computer game. But this time he wasn't playing on the iPad, he was *really* there, charging through the thick mud, stepping over dead bodies whilst trying to dodge bullets from sniper fire.

Real fear coursed through his brain. He expected to be shot dead any second.

He charged on, his heart beating so fast he felt it would burst. He saw the machine-gun post ahead, perched on top of the high trench which marked the front line. He had to get to it...to save the remaining men in his regiment from certain death.

He stormed forward, stopping just short of the machine-gun post. Taking out a grenade from the ammunition pack slung around his neck, he was just about to pull out the pin and hurl it towards the gun slit when suddenly a German soldier ran out from the trench and charged at him with a raised bayonet.

Josh froze. His courage evaporated and he remained rooted to the spot. His enemy screamed at him and thrust the lethal bayonet towards his chest.

Josh prepared to die...*and woke up!*

He sat up in bed, sweat dripping from his forehead. He unbuttoned his pyjama top and examined his chest, half expecting to see a horrible wound.

But there was nothing!

It was all a dream; a horrible nightmare. But it felt so real.

He lay back down and tried to relax...get his mind on what really mattered...his new school tomorrow morning. Suddenly, the idea of starting a new school didn't worry him at all. Compared to being on that battlefield it would be a piece of cake. And then he thought again for a moment...

...Or would it?

FIRST DAY

'This is it then, kiddiewinks,' Mrs Palmer said jovially. 'New term, new school, new beginning.'

'I'm looking forward to it,' Jess said enthusiastically.

Josh stayed silent. He stared to his left out of the passenger side window.

'What about you, Josh? How do you feel?' Mrs Palmer asked her son.

Josh still didn't say anything.

'He's too busy looking at the poppies, Mum,' Jess teased. 'Who says boys don't like flowers!'

Mrs Palmer glanced over to where Josh was staring. 'Hmmm. They're still very impressive. You'd think they'd be dying back by now.'

Josh couldn't take his eyes off them. The side of the car park was still a sea of blood-red flowers. They seemed

29

to stand erect, proud...screaming at Josh to look at them, admire them...*walk over to them!*

Mrs Palmer steered the car into the drop-off zone and brought the car to a halt. As she pulled on the handbrake the car jolted slightly, snapping Josh out of his trance-like state.

'Sorry, Mum. What did you say?'

'Oh, never mind,' Mrs Palmer sighed. 'In a world of your own as usual. Please try and concentrate on your first day, Josh. You need to listen to what people are saying. You might be in Year 6 but bear in mind that you and your sister are very much the 'new kids on the block'.'

Josh glanced over his shoulder and gave Jess a 'knowing look'. She gave him a 'knowing look' back. They always did this when Mum used one of her 'cool phrases'!

A few minutes later the twins were striding towards the school entrance and joining the crowd of excited pupils ready to start their first day back at school.

Jess glanced over her shoulder and gulped nervously as her mother's car disappeared into the distance. Josh took a final glance over *his* shoulder, but more towards the mass of red flowers; he gulped nervously, too...but he wasn't sure why!

*

Three hundred and ninety pupils sat in the Junior Hall for the 'Welcome Back To School' Key Stage 2 Assembly. Years 3 to 5 sat on the floor in rows, but Josh and Jess, along with the rest of Year 6, were privileged to sit on benches at the back. Josh felt very grown up. By the look on Jess's face, she felt the same.

A familiar lady wearing a smart cream jacket over a blue floral dress and carrying a clipboard under her arm made her way to the front of the hall and smiled at them.

'My name's Miss Robinson and I'm the head teacher. I want to welcome you all back after the summer holiday, and an especially warm welcome to the new juniors amongst us...that is all those sitting in front of me in Year 3...'

Josh watched as Miss Robinson cast a beaming smile along each of the two front rows.

'...And to our two new pupils in Year 6 sitting at the back – Josh and Jess Palmer. May I say it's lovely to have twins in the school again.'

Josh stared down at his feet with embarrassment. He cast a quick glance sideways at Jess...she was smiling and lapping up all the attention...*as usual!*

The head teacher continued:

'Please be sure to make our new pupils feel at home and give them all the help and support they need. Remember that Pheasant Bank Academy is a friendly and caring school – first and foremost!'

Josh sat patiently as the head teacher went on for a little longer before ending her speech. A few other teachers then took to the front and introduced themselves before going through a few rules and routines. Finally, an athletic-looking teacher introduced himself as Mr Schofield and Josh noted that the Year 6s sat up a little more attentively; he did the same.

'Those of you already familiar with Pheasant Bank Academy know that we always have a theme for the first

31

term of the new academic year...and this term our theme will be...'World War 1'.'

Josh almost fell backwards off his bench.

Mr Schofield continued, 'Some of you will have noted that the school display boards lining the corridors are empty. Well, I'm relying on you all to help me rectify that! I'm hoping that very soon those boards will be packed with information, artwork and all forms of memorabilia referring to the Great War.'

As Josh tried to contain his excitement, a hand shot up somewhere near the front. 'What does memo... memorab...?'

Mr Schofield smiled a warm smile. '*Memorabilia* means things to do with memories of the great event, Sarah. Your teacher will explain more, I'm sure.'

The teacher paused and scanned the audience. 'Can I just ask how many of you think this will be an interesting topic?'

Almost every hand in the hall went up. Josh put his hand up so fast that he felt a twinge in his shoulder. He looked over to Jess. Her hand was one of the few that stayed down. She had a sad expression on her face.

Mr Schofield looked towards the back of the hall. 'It's interesting to see that our two new Year 6s may be twins but they are of divided opinion. Would you mind telling us, Josh, why you seem so excited about our theme?'

Josh forgot all about his first-day nerves. His mind flashed to the action-packed images within his favourite computer game – Front Line 1.

'Simple, Sir. Lots of heroes, guns and battles. Soldiers charging through the mud and killing the enemy to get to the front line. Proving that the British are the best!'

Some of the Year 6s nodded and smiled at Josh. Mr Schofield nodded too and looked impressed, but Josh noted that *he* didn't smile.

'And what about you, Jess? What are your thoughts? Boring maybe?'

'Not boring, Sir,' Jess replied confidently. 'Just sad. I know we won the war, but why did so many people have to die?'

A hush fell over the hall.

Josh looked straight at Mr Schofield. The teacher was nodding again, but with great sadness in his expression. And then the teacher looked across at Jess...and smiled.

*

Josh's first day in his new school was going from strength to strength. Not only was the school's World War 1 theme Josh's dream, but it turned out that the teacher-in-charge, Mr Schofield, was Head of Year 6, the school's specialist History teacher...and his and Jess's form tutor!

Brilliant!

Josh noted that not everyone in his new form was quite so enthusiastic.

'Why didn't you pick World War 2 as our theme, Sir?' a boy with a tired expression asked Mr Schofield. 'Surely World War 1 was too long ago?'

'But not too long ago for us to ever forget, Sam,' the teacher replied. 'That's exactly why our World War 1 theme *is* so important...to keep the memory alive. So many people died during the war, we owe it to them, and to ourselves, to remember them.'

A girl sitting quite near to Josh, and next to his twin sister, raised her hand.

'Yes, Millie?'

'Is there anyone still alive who fought in World War 1?'

Mr Schofield turned his attention to her. 'The Great War took place from 1914 to 1918, Millie. Any 18-year-old soldier – and they *were* as young as 18 – who survived the war would have to be around 120 years old if they were still alive.'

'Maybe some of our grandfathers fought in the war,' Josh asked, his mind swirling with thoughts.

Jess's hand shot into the air. 'It would have to be our *great* grandfather, wouldn't it, Sir?'

'Almost, Jess,' the teacher said. 'It would actually have to be your *great-great-* grandfather.'

'Like I said,' the boy at the back of the class piped up again, stifling a yawn, '...it's ancient history.'

Josh glanced across at his sister. He could see by her face she was working things out. Her hand went up again. 'Sir, would that be your grandfather's grandfather?'

Mr Schofield looked impressed. 'That's exactly right, Jess.' He turned to the class. 'And that's why if any of you are lucky enough to have a grandfather, you might just ask them if they remember *their* grandfather being involved in any way with the Great War. They may even have something handed down to them. I have an uncle who passed on to me a set of medals. They were left to him by his grandmother. Her husband was a hero who died in action.'

Josh's eyes grew wide. 'That's amazing, Sir,' he found himself saying out loud. 'By the way, I've got a real World War 1 helmet.'

'Really, Josh? Maybe you could bring it in to show everyone?'

'He'll do more than that, Sir,' Jess piped up confidently. 'He'll tell you everything you need to know about it.'

'Well, we'll look forward to it,' Mr Schofield said kindly. 'But now we must move on to our Science lesson.' He turned to the interactive white board and wrote on it in big letters:

BOTANY

'Anyone tell me what this word means?'

Josh guessed whose hand would go up first. He was right.

'Plants, Sir. It's the science of plants and flowers.'

'Well done, Jess. That's correct. And today, to fit in with our Great War theme, we're going to take a look at a particular flower...' He went over to the computer on his desk, clicked on the mouse and the striking image of a blood-red flower sprang up on the interactive white board, complete with its name below it:

FIELD POPPY

Latin name – *Papaver rhoeas*

At the mention of 'poppy', Josh felt compelled to look to his left out through the classroom window.

...His blood ran cold!

There in the distance, he could just see the tops of the poppies by the side of the car park...*and among them the ghostly shimmering figure of a soldier.*

He turned towards his sister, trying desperately to

grab her attention. Sometimes, if he concentrated hard enough, she would turn towards him. But not this time. She was too intent on listening to Mr Schofield.

His heart still racing, he turned back towards the window and stared across at the poppies...*the figure had disappeared.*

BACKING OFF

Josh knocked on his sister's bedroom door. KNOCK…
KNOCK, KNOCK.

'Enter,' she called out from inside.

He walked in and sat heavily on the end of Jess's bed.
She was sitting at her desk, already engrossed in the little
bit of homework they'd been set.

Typical of Jess!

He glanced around her room, so very different
from his own. Everything was unpacked and arranged
immaculately. Since the move, some of Josh's things were
still in boxes and shoved under his bed.

'Do you know *why* poppies are a symbol of the war?'
he asked.

Jess carried on writing. 'Not until Mr Schofield told
us. I just knew that people wear them on Remembrance

Sunday.'

'Exactly. Everybody knows that. But I didn't know why until today.'

Jess still didn't look up from her homework. 'Because they were the first flowers to spring up in the battlefields after the war was over. Especially in France.'

'Yeah. Poppies like to grow on waste ground,' Josh said. 'I did a bit of research on my own after Mr Schofield got me interested.'

Jess laughed. 'Josh Palmer interested in poppies! A-mazing!'

'Well, guess what? I looked out of the classroom window today and saw a soldier standing in the poppies,' he said casually, glancing at Jess's posters arranged neatly around the walls.

She stopped what she was doing and swivelled around on her seat to look back at him. 'I'm starting to worry about you, Josh. You've been really weird since we moved here. Now you're seeing things! Maybe that war game you keep playing is getting to you. You need to cut down a bit.'

Josh looked thoughtful. 'Maybe you're right. Maybe I need to give the whole war thing a bit of a break. I even found myself asking some of the kids today if they'd ever heard of that dry cleaners.'

Jess frowned at her brother. 'Oh yeah. *Warners*. And had they?'

Josh shook his head. 'Nope...no one! I stopped asking in the end 'cause I started getting some weird looks.'

Jess turned her attention back to her homework. 'Like you said, Bro, forget about the Great War for a bit and maybe things will calm down.'

Josh made his way back to his own room. He decided to follow his sister's advice and get straight on with his homework. Get it out of the way and relax a little. Forget about the strange things that had happened. Concentrate on settling into his new school and making new friends.

He sat down at his desk. It was identical to his sister's. Mum had got the two of them for a bargain in a furniture sale. Only Jess's desk was always tidy, everything neatly arranged and in its place.

...Unlike Josh's desk! Every drawer stuffed with all manner of things and the surface covered in random piles of books and papers, all scattered around his laptop.

He looked at the laptop. He tried to resist.

...But he couldn't!

A few minutes later the laptop was switched on and he'd put the name of the dry cleaners into the search provider.

Why didn't I think of that before!

The name came up immediately:

WARNERS DRY CLEANERS

Three branches in Manchester

Josh scanned the info on the dry-cleaning shops and found the three addresses. He made a note of them and set off to tell Jess. But then he stopped himself.

It could wait until tomorrow.

Maybe even wait until the weekend. Like Jess said, it was time to back off and let things settle down.

He rooted out his homework, spread it on his desk and got on with it. Half an hour later it was finished. When he put his mind to it, he knew he could work to a good standard...it was all a matter of concentration!

He put things away and packed his school bag ready for tomorrow. Just before heading downstairs to watch some TV, he glanced back at the laptop.

Maybe just one little game of Front Line 1...

But he decided to resist temptation. He bit into his bottom lip, clenched his fists and made his way downstairs.

*

The next morning Josh ate his breakfast and felt good about himself. He'd slept better than any night since they'd moved in, no doubt due to the fact that he'd managed to close his mind to anything and everything associated with the Great War.

Passing through the school gates that morning, he even managed to avert his eyes from looking at the sea of poppies...never even crossed his mind!

'Are you OK, Josh?' Mrs Palmer asked with surprise in her voice. 'I thought you'd be back on the iPad by now, blasting the enemy to pieces!'

'Too much other stuff going on,' Josh replied brightly. 'We've got football today. Can't wait.'

'Ooohh...get him!' Mrs Palmer laughed. 'Growing up fast...will it last?'

Josh looked over his shoulder and gave Jess a knowing look. She grinned back at him.

A short while later, Viking Class were ready for their Science lesson with Mr Schofield.

'It's time we got some material for our themed display,' the teacher informed the pupils. He walked over to the classroom window and looked out. The sun was shining.

'We're going to head out across the playground to the poppies.'

Josh gulped. *Here we go again! Just when I'd got my mind off them!*

'When we get over there, I'll show you how to select one ready for pressing.'

'How do you press them?' a familiar voice asked impatiently.

'...And when we get back, Millie, I'll show you how to press them! Believe me, they'll look impressive and add greatly to our display.'

Mr Schofield lined the class up by the door and began leading them out. Josh glanced at his sister. She looked back at him with an expression of concern on her face. As they made their way across the playground, Josh felt his heart beat fast. He stared ahead towards the poppies, half-expecting to see the image of the ghostly soldier staring back at him.

...But there was nothing but blood-red flowers. All was calm and peaceful.

Just as it should be!

Mr Schofield led his class to the edge of the poppy embankment. He stooped down and felt the ground. It was dry, so he beckoned the class to sit down. He stood in front of them and held a pair of scissors aloft. 'Choose a poppy in good condition and cut the stem as near to the ground as you can. Leaving the root in the ground means that the poppy plant can produce more flowers. The scissors are in this tray. Work in pairs. One of you can come and get the scissors as soon as I give the word.' The teacher looked up at the clear blue sky and smiled. 'It's a lovely morning and it's good to be outside in the fresh air.'

Somewhere high above, several crows circled and cawed.

And then a different sound.

Despite there being no wind, somewhere behind the teacher, the surface of the poppies rustled.

It was Millie who broke the ominous silence. 'Sir... why are the poppies moving behind you?'

Josh felt a shiver run down his spine.

There *was* a rustling from behind the teacher. And worse...there was a line of disturbance in the poppies heading straight towards them.

Mr Schofield swung round as the disturbance reached his feet and stumbled backwards as something shot up into the air with a shrill scream. Everyone in Viking Class yelled out in shocked surprise.

...And then they all laughed.

Mr Schofield laughed too. 'Oh well. We're not called Pheasant Bank Academy for nothing.'

As the strikingly coloured bird fluttered away into the distance, Mr Schofield explained that the pheasants from which the school had taken its name originated from the days in which the land had been an estate.

'They used to shoot them, Sir, didn't they?' one of the boys asked with interest.

'Yes...that's right,' Mr Schofield replied. 'They bred them from chicks and shot them for sport.'

'Poor sport in my opinion,' Jess muttered loud enough for everyone to hear. 'They're beautiful birds and should be left well alone.'

Josh suddenly found himself needing to get back into school. He raised his hand and asked permission to go to the toilet.

'Quick as you can, Josh,' Mr Schofield said. 'We need to cut these poppies and get back inside to the project in hand.'

Josh jogged back across the car park and into school. He headed down the main corridor towards the boys' toilets...and stopped dead in his tracks!

A chill rattled down his spine as his nose picked up the distinct smell of pipe tobacco.

STRANGE HAPPENINGS

Josh crept on down the school corridor, the aromatic smell of pipe tobacco growing stronger with every step. His heart was beating fast, his ears straining to pick up sounds.

But all was silent...*too* silent!

His brain told him that in addition to the teachers there were easily around 400 pupils in the school, so why couldn't he hear a single sound? With his senses on full alert, he tiptoed on towards the end of the corridor. The toilets were just around the corner.

He stopped, his heart racing faster than ever. He thought he could hear something...just ahead of him...a shuffling sound.

...Like someone was waiting for him.

He thought about turning back. Did he really need

44

the toilet? *Yes,* he did. In fact he needed the toilet badly.

Only one thing for it! I'm going to count up to three.

With the smell of tobacco filling his nostrils and more shuffling sounds reaching his ears, Josh braced himself and took a deep breath.

One, two, three...

'JOSH! WHAT'S WRONG? YOU LOOK LOST!'

Josh swung round. It was Miss Robinson, the head teacher, standing behind him at the far end of the corridor. He walked back towards her. 'Sorry. I couldn't remember where the toilets were.'

She smiled warmly at him. 'Oh, Josh. You were almost there. They're just around the corner from where you were standing. Come on. I'm heading that way myself.'

Josh relaxed a little as Miss Robinson led the way. As they turned the corner, he noted that the smell of pipe tobacco had disappeared. And there was no one there!

He thanked her, shot in and out of the toilet faster than he'd ever done in his entire life and was soon back with his class again, kneeling among the poppies with Mr Schofield watching over them.

'Are you OK, Josh?' Jess whispered in his ear. 'You look like you've seen a ghost.'

'I think I nearly did,' he replied mysteriously. 'I'll tell you later.'

Jess handed him a pair of scissors and he scanned around for a really striking poppy. It didn't take long to find one – there were so many. He did as Mr Schofield had told them and cut the stem as low down as possible to just where it met the ground.

A few minutes later and Mr Schofield was leading the

class back into school, each of them holding their plant specimens as gently as possible.

'We'll get these pressed as soon as we get back inside,' the teacher shouted over his shoulder.

Josh was at the back of the line. He looked down at the blood-red flower in his hand. It was the most brilliant red he'd ever seen.

...And yet it made him feel sad.

A tear trickled down his cheek. He felt embarrassed and quickly brushed it away.

Walking towards the main entrance, Josh glanced over his shoulder towards the poppies.

The ghostly image was back.

...But this time it was much clearer. A soldier with a rifle slung over his shoulder.

As Josh stood rooted to the spot, gawping at the tall shimmering figure, it raised a ghostly hand and waved at him.

He turned to the others to see if anyone else had seen it. But they were all inside already.

The door opened and Jess's face appeared. 'Come on, slowcoach. What's keeping you?'

Josh was speechless. He turned his head, ready to point out the ghostly soldier to his sister. But there was nothing there. *Vanished!*

'Josh! What's wrong with you?' Jess snapped at him. 'Look what you've done.'

She was staring down at his hand. Josh followed her gaze and saw that he'd crushed the beautiful crimson flower in his clenched fist. He looked up at his sister with big eyes. He didn't know what to say.

'Josh...what's wrong with you?' she said softly. 'You're crying!'

*

That night Josh told his sister everything. She sat on the end of his bed and listened with interest. When Josh had finished, she nodded her head solemnly.

'I've been getting some spooky vibes, too,' she said.

'That figures. We're twins, aren't we?'

'Suppose so. But my vibes don't compare to your spooky experiences. Even so, I think it proves there's deffo something weird going on.'

'So are you going to help me get to the bottom of this?' Josh asked his sister.

Jess looked thoughtful. She nodded. 'That creepy face on your laptop. It's got to be a clue to all this. You said the woman was standing in front of a war memorial by the side of that dry cleaners.'

'Yeah. *Warners*. It's in Manchester. Remember...I checked the name out on the internet.'

'Exactly,' Jess said. 'And who do you think knows Manchester better than anyone?'

Josh sat bolt upright on his bed. 'Grandad!'

'Exactly,' Jess repeated. 'Mum says we're going to visit him at the weekend. He'll know where it is. Then we can go over there and see exactly what that woman was staring at.'

'Before she started staring at *me*,' he reminded his sister. 'OMG, Jess. You should have seen her eyes. They really freaked me out.'

47

As Jess left his room, he glanced over to his desk.

His laptop was open and the light from the screen was willing him to go over...to load up his favourite game... Front Line 1. Maybe he could just have one more go before bed. He just had to get to the front line and reach Level 3; take out the machine gun post and find out what lay beyond the enemy trench.

...Within minutes Josh found himself heavily into the game. He was soon out of his own trench, clambering over the top and charging across the boggy, barren battlefield. Soldiers were falling all around him, some his own men, some the enemy.

Sounds of big guns rattled out from the laptop's speaker system...BOOM! BOOM! BOOM!

Sounds of rifle fire...CRACK! CRACK! CRACK!

Sounds of grenades, one landing close by and blowing up one of his comrades...BANG!!

Josh took his avatar onwards, skirting around bomb craters and dodging enemy gunfire, easily conquering Levels 1 and 2. Once again the enemy machine gun post loomed before him, the only thing between him and Level 3.

He'd taken it out last time with a single grenade, just before the power had cut off and that weird thing had happened.

This time...nothing would stop him!

...But something was willing him to turn around. He paused the game, turned in his seat and saw the World War 1 helmet on the floor just beneath his bed. He went over, picked it up and put it on.

Yes!

Now he felt even more like a *real* soldier. This would surely help him concentrate even harder. Take out the machine-gun post and reach Level 3.

He sat back at his desk, tapped a key and stared at the screen. As the game resumed, smoke bellowed from a crater as another enemy bomb exploded to the left of the screen.

But this time he could smell it!

And as another bomb exploded even closer, the little figure under Josh's control fell over from the blast.

And Josh was 'blown' backwards off his seat.

As he landed heavily on the bedroom floor, the smell of acrid smoke filled his nostrils. All went black and his mind swirled as the sounds of the battlefield rang in his ears. He felt a searing pain and realised the helmet had dug into the front of his head as he'd fallen. With his eyes closed, trying desperately to shut out the horror of what was happening, he touched his forehead and felt the warmness of the blood running from a deep cut.

'Josh...whatever's happened?'

Mrs Palmer appeared. She helped him to sit up and removed the helmet at the same time.

He opened his eyes. 'I don't know, Mum.'

The pain had gone. No cut, no blood. No smoke, no smells. Everything was back to normal. Josh couldn't believe it!

Mrs Palmer looked at Josh's desk. 'It's that computer game again, isn't it?' she said sternly. 'I think it's time you gave it a rest. I'm beginning to think this whole war thing is beginning to get to you.'

Josh nodded and rose to his feet.

Mrs Palmer walked back to the door. 'And by the way,' she said, turning back towards him, 'don't forget we're going to see Grandad George on Saturday, so don't make any plans.'

'OK, Mum...no problem. He didn't fight in the Great War did he, Mum?'

Before Mrs Palmer had a chance to reply, a familiar voice sounded from the doorway. 'No, but I'm guessing his grandfather did,' Jess said knowingly.

'Oh, here we go,' Mrs Palmer sighed. 'Back to the war again! You can ask him about it, but I seem to remember your father saying it's a subject he's not too keen to talk about.'

Josh fell silent and stared at his sister. She had that determined look in her eyes...the one he'd come to recognise and rely on whenever things got tough!

GRANDAD GEORGE

The weekend couldn't come fast enough for Josh.

Though nothing else untoward had happened at school, he'd become distinctly nervous of being around the place, especially on his own. Trips to the toilet during lessons were out of the question – the smell of pipe tobacco and strange shuffling sounds from around corners had made their mark!

'Are you two ready?' Mrs Palmer called out from the kitchen.

'Yep...we're good to go.' Jess answered for the two of them.

Josh checked his backpack for the third time – World War 1 helmet, school jotter in case he needed to make any notes, a few sweets, a can of fizzy drink and a few other bits and pieces. The helmet and the jotter were the main things; the other stuff wasn't really important. 'Is Dad coming with us?' Josh asked his sister.

Mum appeared from the kitchen and answered for her. 'No. He's going to take advantage of the peace and quiet and catch up on some paperwork.'

Dad's face appeared, poking around the corner from the hallway. 'Sorry, kids. I've got loads to catch up on, what with it being a new job and such. Give my regards to Grandad George and tell him I'll see him soon. He'll no doubt be pleased to see you...and who knows...he might even be in a good mood for once!'

Though Mr Palmer was laughing as he headed back upstairs, Josh knew his dad was only too right. Grandad George rarely raised a smile these days – ever since Grandma Joyce had died. But he was still their grandad and he and Jess loved him dearly.

...And right now Josh had some serious questions to ask him.

He picked up his backpack and headed towards the door. Jess and Mum followed, and it wasn't long before they were motoring along the M62 and over the moors towards Manchester.

*

Mrs Palmer turned the corner into Mangham Terrace and carefully manoeuvred the white hatchback into a space just outside number 12.

Josh looked out of the passenger-side window across to the house and saw the curtains move. As they got out of the car, the door to the little terraced house opened and

Grandad George was standing on the doorstep waiting to greet them.

'How was the journey?' he called down the neatly-paved pathway.

'Nice and quiet!' Mrs Palmer called back to him. 'Hardly a lorry in sight.'

'And what about the terrible twins?' he said as the three of them made their way towards him. 'Were *they* quiet?'

Josh noted the faintest of smiles on his Grandad's face.

'Hardly said a word,' Mrs Palmer replied in a surprised tone of voice. 'Even Jess seems a bit subdued this morning.'

'Well it's good to see you. Come on in. I've already got the kettle on.'

They entered the hallway. Mrs Palmer closed the door as Josh and Jess kicked off their shoes and followed Grandad George into the front room. Like the rest of the house, the sitting room was neat and tidy and had a clean scented smell about it. Grandma Joyce had always taken great pride in looking after No.12 Mangham Terrace and, since losing her, Grandad George had kept the house to the same high standard.

After a brief chat and explaining why Dad wasn't with them, Mrs Palmer disappeared with Grandad George into the kitchen to prepare drinks and snacks.

Josh started unpacking his backpack.

'When are you going to ask him?' Jess whispered loudly.

'Soon as he comes back in. The sooner the better.' He took out the helmet and placed it on the rug. He was just taking out his school jotter complete with a few scribbled notes when Grandad reappeared carrying a tray of drinks. Mum followed with a tray of snacks.

'By God! Where did you get that?' Grandad asked, nodding towards the steel helmet. The tray wavered and rattled as he spoke and he had to put it down quickly.

'In a charity shop,' Jess answered for Josh.

'It's a World War 1 helmet,' Josh informed him. 'It's made of steel and it's...'

'I know what it is,' Grandad interrupted harshly. 'I just don't know why you would want it. Wars are best forgotten.' He sat down heavily in his armchair and looked thoughtful.

Mrs Palmer passed Grandad George a steaming mug of tea and offered him a digestive biscuit. 'Sorry, George! I did mention to them that you don't like to talk about the Great War.' She turned towards Josh and frowned. 'I suppose he's just a normal boy. Obsessed with war games and killing the enemy, like most other kids.'

Grandad George forced a smile. 'You're right. When *we* were kids, we used to charge around outside with a wooden gun and a colander on our head. I suppose now it's all done on computers.'

'Dead right, Grandad,' Jess chipped in. 'And 'dead' is the right word...Josh isn't happy unless he's surrounded by dead bodies.'

'Yeah...but only the enemy's dead bodies,' Josh added defensively. He glanced across at Jess and then back to Grandad. 'Did you fight in the war, Grandad?'

'Not old enough,' he replied, shaking his head.

'What about Great-Grandad?' Jess asked him, glancing at Josh.

'Still not old enough. It was *my* grandad, that's your great-great-grandad Stanley, that fought in the First World War. But your mum's right. I'd rather not talk about it.'

He took a bite of his biscuit along with a sip of tea.

Mrs Palmer quickly changed the subject to their recent move and talked about their new house. It was when they began talking about their 'new town' that Josh saw the opportunity for his next 'big' question:

'Somebody at school said there's a really cool burger bar called WARNERS! Is there one in Manchester, Grandad?'

Grandad George looked thoughtful and shook his head. 'The only WARNERS I know is the dry cleaners down by the park.'

Jess beamed. 'Oh...is that the park where you used to take us to the swings and slides when we were younger?'

Mum nodded. 'You used to love it there.'

'I wouldn't mind checking it out,' Josh said. 'I remember it really well.'

Grandad George got up from his chair and walked over to the window. 'The sun's shining. Why don't you two have a wander down there and leave me and your mum to have a chat in peace for an hour or so. When you get back, we'll have some lunch ready.'

'...And give your grandad some rest from all this talk about war and such,' Mrs Palmer added sternly.

Josh grinned at his sister. She grinned back. *Things were going well!*

*

The twins turned the corner of Mangham Terrace and headed towards the playing fields. The park was on the far side of the fields. They remembered the park so well, but neither of them could remember much about the shopping precinct by the side of it.

'Did you see his face when he saw the helmet?' Jess asked her brother.

'I know! It really upset him.'

'Yeah...but why?'

Josh shook his head. 'I've no idea. It's so mysterious. And yet...do you know what, Jess. I've got a really strong feeling that we're going to find out.'

Jess strode on, Josh almost having to trot to keep up with her. 'And do *you* know what, Bro...' she said looking straight ahead, '...I've got the same feeling.'

THE WAR MEMORIAL

It being Saturday morning, the park was busy with lots of families and young children. As they approached the recreation ground, the memories came flooding back.

'Do you remember, Josh? You were always afraid of the big slide,' Jess teased.

'And *you* were afraid of nothing!' Josh replied. 'I spent my whole life trying to keep up with you.'

They both laughed out loud and walked on. A busy road ran alongside the recreation ground, and they crossed it towards the shopping precinct visible in the distance.

Josh broke into a trot and pointed forward. 'I think I can see it...the War Memorial. I'm sure it's the same one I saw on the computer.'

Jess put a spurt on to keep up with her brother and sounded even more excited. 'And I've just spotted something else!'

'What?'

She pointed beyond the marble column. 'The dry cleaners.'

Josh gasped. 'I see it!'

The shop sign was striking with blue lettering on a white background – WARNERS. It was no surprise that it had stood out from the other shops.

Josh walked slowly up to the memorial and saw the list of names etched onto the marble column and the wreaths of poppies laid at its base. In fact everything looked the same as he'd seen on his laptop. The only thing missing was the spooky veiled lady standing in front of it.

Jess walked up by his side. 'Didn't you say there was someone with our name?'

Josh nodded. 'There was deffo a Palmer...I think it was Stanley.'

'OMG! That was *his* name!'

'Who?'

'Our great, great grandfather...don't you remember what Grandad said? Grandad's grandad!'

Josh turned to his sister with wide eyes. 'That's right!' He turned back to the marble column and scanned quickly down the list of names to the Ps:

MARK NOBLE

GEORGE ALFRED ORMKIRK

JAMES PHILIP POLLARD

ROBERT PULLMAN...

'It's not there!' Josh exclaimed, his voice full of frustration. 'But it has to be! This is definitely the place and I deffo saw the name. I'm sure it was Stanley...a middle name...and Palmer.'

'Well it's not there now, little brother.'

'Hey, less of the 'little'!' Josh said grumpily. 'Just because you were born seven minutes before me.'

Jess put her arm around Josh's shoulder and steered him back towards the park. 'OK...but just to prove we *are* equal, you can join me on the big slide...one last go. Come on, I'll race you!'

Josh's mind suddenly flashed to Front Line 1. He pushed Jess to one side and sprinted off towards the recreation ground. If he was going to take out a machine-gun post, get to Level 3 and go beyond the front line, then there was no way he could be afraid of a big slide anymore.

Bring it on, big sister...bring it on!

*

Josh raced up the path of 12 Mangham Terrace. He reached out to push on the doorbell, but the door was already opening. Mrs Palmer stood there with a solemn look on her face.

'Hi, Mum. Is something wrong?' Josh asked.

"Mum!' Jess joined in. 'You look stressed.'

'Come in and see for yourselves,' was all Mrs Palmer said.

The twins followed her down the hallway into the sitting room. Grandad George was sitting in his usual chair, cradling Josh's war helmet in his lap and staring into space.

'Hi, Grandad!' Jess called out cheerily. 'The park was

great. Josh even dared to go on the big slide!'

There was no response. Grandad George just stared back with sad eyes.

'What's wrong with him, Mum?' Josh asked, joining his sister on the sofa.

Mrs Palmer remained standing and looked from Grandad to the two of them. 'I can't understand it. He was fine until about an hour ago. We were chatting away about this and that...and then he reached down and picked up the helmet from where Josh had left it on the carpet.'

Josh stiffened. 'Then what happened?'

Mrs Palmer stroked her hand over her brow. 'Well...he was sort of looking at it...moving it around in his hands. And then he froze. And he's been sitting there ever since with that strange look in his eyes.'

Josh walked over to Grandad George, reached down and tried to take the helmet from him. 'It's OK, Grandad. It's just an old helmet.'

At first Josh couldn't prize the helmet out of his hands. But slowly Grandad George's fingers released their vice-like grip and Josh took the helmet away from him. At the same time the old man's eyes blinked back to awareness.

'George! Are you OK?' Mrs Palmer asked with concern.

He nodded and stared up into Josh's eyes. 'I can't believe it! It's not just an old war helmet,' he said sadly. 'It's *his* helmet!'

Josh had no idea what his grandad was talking about. He tapped on the helmet's steel surface; it made a ringing sound.

Grandad George reached out and Josh passed it back to him. Mrs Palmer and the twins watched with curiosity as Grandad George turned the helmet over and pointed inside. His hands trembled as he spoke. 'Like I said...it's *his*. He's come back to haunt us.'

'George! You're frightening the kids now! What're you talking about? Give it here!'

She took the helmet from her father-in-law, turned it over, and examined the underside. 'I can't see much. Oh wait...there's some sort of lettering. Someone must have scribbled it in years ago. It's almost faded away....S...O...P.'

Josh peered into the helmet. 'Yes...I spotted it before and showed it to Jess.'

'We guessed it might be the owner of the helmet,' Jess added.

'You're right. It was *his*,' Grandad George said with a little more firmness in his voice. 'Stanley Oswald Palmer.'

Josh's mind reeled. The name on the war memorial... the one he'd seen on the computer screen:

...STANLEY OSWALD PALMER

'And now it's not there,' he found himself saying out loud. 'It *was* on the war memorial...but now it's not.'

'What *are* you on about?' Mrs Palmer asked, shaking her head.

It was Grandad George who answered. 'Course it's not on the war memorial. Why would it be? He was a coward!'

Josh swallowed hard as he saw the tears streaming down his grandad's cheeks, his expression a dreadful mix of shame and rage.

*

As Mrs Palmer drove back home over the Pennines, the atmosphere in the car was subdued. At first no one spoke. It was Jess who eventually broke the silence.

'Grandad looked so sad,' she said glumly.

'And so angry,' Mrs Palmer added, shaking her head. 'Even so...I can't believe he reacted like that.'

'What do you think he meant?' Josh joined in. '... About our great-great-grandad Stanley being a coward... and his name not being on the war memorial.'

'I've no idea,' Mrs Palmer said firmly. 'And I don't really want to know. Like your grandad says, the war is best forgotten.'

'It's not easy to forget when it's our theme for the term,' Josh reminded her.

'Well, I'm not saying it should be forgotten altogether,' Mrs Palmer stated. 'We owe it to those who died for us to remember. Especially on Remembrance Day. I'll be wearing my poppy just like everyone else.'

'November 11th,' Jess chipped in. 'At eleven o'clock.'

The mention of 'poppies' made Josh feel uneasy. For the rest of the journey he remained quiet, thinking about everything that had happened. A couple of times he glanced over his shoulder at Jess. Her eyes were closed, but he guessed she wasn't asleep. He knew that she was going over everything in *her* mind, just as he was.

BACK TO 'NORMAL'

The next week passed without incident and everything seemed quite normal.

The Great War theme at Pheasant Bank Academy continued and the display boards filled up with some amazing artwork and writing from pupils of all ages. And, with no more 'spooky incidents' taking place, Josh began to wonder if all that stuff with Grandad George and the War Memorial had really happened! If it wasn't for Jess still going on about it, he might just have to put it down to an over-active imagination brought on by his favourite computer game.

By the weekend things were so normal that Josh decided to get back to Front Line 1 and try to get to Level 3. He checked that the war helmet was safely tucked away under his bed. No way was he wearing that again...at least not when playing Front Line 1!

Within minutes Josh had his avatar charging across the battlefield, skilfully dodging bullets, avoiding bomb craters and heading at speed towards the machine-gun post. Despite it being over a week since he'd played, he'd lost none of his expertise and still remembered how to get hold of a grenade at just the right moment and hurl it with great accuracy towards the enemy gunner.

BOOM!

The machine-gun post crumbled and Josh advanced his small figure towards the enemy trench.

This is it! Level 3, here I come!

Without warning, two German soldiers emerged out of the enemy trench and charged at him with raised bayonets...but Josh shot them dead.

I'm there! I'm there!

...But a siren sounded from the computer followed by two words flashing on the screen:

GAS ATTACK! GAS ATTACK!

Josh couldn't believe it. He watched open-mouthed as his avatar fell to the ground...GAME OVER!

It was only then he noticed that some of the surviving British soldiers were wearing gas masks.

So that's the answer!

Josh now realised what he had to do to advance the last few metres, to reach the enemy trench and get to Level 3.

...But he felt tired and decided it would have to wait until next time.

That night, in bed, Josh tossed and turned. His mind wrestled with a question that he just couldn't get out of his mind:

When he finally got to Level 3 and advanced beyond the enemy trench, what would he find and what would happen next?

*

Monday morning and Mrs Palmer slowed the car as she turned through the school gates. Josh glanced out at the poppies. No longer the intense blood-red canvas; now more a wash of faded pink, invoking a sense of withering and dying. He felt a tinge of sadness at the sight of them.

'OK, you two,' Mrs Palmer said. 'See you later. Have a good day.'

Josh and Jess got out of the car and headed over towards the school building.

'You're very quiet,' Jess said to her brother.

'I know,' Josh replied. 'I've got a strange feeling.'

'...That something weird's going to happen again?'

'Exactly!' Josh confirmed. 'Have you got it, too?'

Jess nodded solemnly and walked on.

First lesson was with their form tutor, Mr Schofield. He chatted to the class about how well the Great War theme was going and how impressed he was by the standard of work displayed on the school notice boards. Josh placed his elbows on his desk and cradled his head in his hands. He felt tired and distracted.

'Today,' Mr Schofield continued, 'we have arranged for someone special to visit us. Our guest will be arriving shortly. I think you're going to find this person *very* interesting.'

Josh stifled a yawn.

'His name is Captain Armstrong. Like I said...you'll find him a fascinating character.'

Josh sat bolt upright. He glanced over at Jess – she had an interested look on her face too.

The music of the National Anthem suddenly sounded from the front of the class. It was the ring tone from Mr Schofield's mobile phone hidden beneath some books on his desk. Some of the pupils giggled.

Mr Schofield put the phone to his ear, muttered something into it and turned to the class. 'Well, it seems our visitor has arrived early and is waiting in Reception. Josh, would you like to go down and escort him back to our class?'

Josh almost fell off his chair.

Why me?

But he said nothing. He didn't even look over to Jess. He simply nodded, made his way out of the classroom and headed down the corridor towards the school office.

Once again, the faint smell of pipe tobacco reached his nostrils and the hackles on the back of his neck stood on end. He stopped for a second...not a sound from anywhere...the school seemed deserted...silent!

...And then a voice from somewhere just ahead of him. 'Is that you, Palmer? Come on in.'

Josh almost jumped out of his skin. He took a few more steps down the deserted corridor and peered through an open door on his left. A man in soldier's uniform sat behind a desk filled with papers. The man had a thin face with hollow cheeks. His skin was as white as snow. His hair was slicked back with a neat parting down one side and he had a thin, perfectly-groomed moustache beneath his nose.

'Don't be shy, Private Palmer,' the soldier said to him. 'Come on in and close the door.'

The penny dropped!

This was Captain Armstrong, the visitor that Mr Schofield had spoken about – an actor playing the part of an officer from the Great War!

Josh breathed more easily. He'd been set up and decided to go along with it. 'Yes, Sir!' he said proudly. He snapped his feet together and stood to attention, giving his finest salute.

The man looked up at him. 'Stand easy, Palmer! Like I said, close the door and take a seat.'

Josh did as he was told. He sat down on the hard wooden chair placed in front of the officer's desk and shivered. The room felt cold...ice-cold. The smell of pipe tobacco was strong. His eyes picked out the pipe leaning on an ashtray among the piles of papers.

'Now then, Private Palmer,' the man began, looking down at a document in front of him. 'You have an excellent record to date; two bouts of action resulting in numerous commendations and now a recommendation for a medal for gallantry from your regiment.' He looked up and gazed into Josh's eyes. 'Damn good show, Palmer.'

'Thank you, Sir,' Josh beamed, going along with the 'act'.

The officer rose to his feet. Josh noted how tall he was...well over six feet. 'As your commanding officer I've recommended you for promotion, Palmer. Seems to me you'll make a fine corporal, and who knows what else after that.'

'Thank you, Sir!' Josh repeated.

'The fact is, Palmer, the Manchester Regiment have a tough assignment coming up.'

Josh gulped and stiffened.

Of all the places to mention...why Manchester!

'Northern France,' the officer continued. 'The enemy are rallying. We need to show strength and push them back.'

Josh's mind was swirling...trying desperately to sort fact from fiction. 'Yes...yes...Sir!' he stammered.

'Very well,' the officer said firmly. 'That's all for now, Palmer. Keep up the good work and send in the next man.'

Josh stood up, clicked his feet together again and saluted. He turned towards the door, opened it and took a final glance back at the officer – he was seated and writing busily. He never even looked up. Josh frowned. He thought the man would have at least smiled at the end of their little game, just to show it *was* only an act.

But why Manchester?... Josh thought to himself again as he made his way back to Viking Class. *That was so weird.*

He walked back into class and looked straight at Mr Schofield. 'Captain Armstrong's ready for the next....' he stopped short.

Mr Schofield was standing at the front with a man by his side. The man looked old and was wearing an army uniform, including a peaked cap on his head. He had a big white moustache and a warm smile on his face. He was quite small and much shorter than Mr Schofield.

'*This* is Captain Armstrong, Josh. He made his own way here. Where on earth did you get to?'

Everyone in Viking Class turned and looked at Josh.

He gazed around at the sea of bemused faces. 'I...I... was just in with my commanding officer, Sir. Taking orders for the next line of attack.'

Everyone burst out laughing. Even Mr Schofield and Captain Armstrong smiled.

But his twin sister, Jess, stared back at him with an expression full of worry and concern. She was the only one in Viking Class who knew that Josh wasn't joking!

DETECTIVES

That night, just before bed, Josh and Jess had a BIG meeting. It was in Josh's room. He lay back on the bed staring at the ceiling and Jess sat at his desk facing him, with her back to his computer.

Josh told Jess everything that had happened in his encounter with the army officer and Jess sat with her arms folded across her chest, listening with an expression of intense concentration.

'And you're sure you didn't imagine all this,' she said when Josh had finished.

'Nope...it was real and it was spooky. The man's face was as white as snow and the room was ice cold. It freaked me out a bit when he called me by my name, Palmer, and then he mentioned Manchester. I *deffo* didn't imagine it!'

Jess nodded solemnly. 'This is all like some sort of

giant jigsaw puzzle. We need to keep cool and try to put the pieces together.'

'You're right, Sis,' Josh said, sitting up on his bed and staring at her. 'And do you know what? I'm sure it's got something to do with our great-grandad and the First World War.'

Jess shook her head and corrected him, 'You mean our great-*great*-grandfather: Stanley Oswald Palmer.'

'Yep,' Josh nodded. 'You're right. Don't you think it was weird the way that Grandad didn't want to talk about him and called him a coward?'

Jess frowned. 'There's been so many weird things happening since we moved here. Look...let's make a list and see if we can make any sense of it.'

Now it was Josh's turn to frown. 'Where do we start?'

'You know your problem...' Jess said firmly. '...You don't watch enough detective programmes. You're too busy playing stupid war games on your PC.' She swivelled round to face Josh's desk, took a blank sheet of paper from the printer and reached for a pencil. 'OK...what's the very first thing that happened?'

'You mean *weird* thing?' Josh asked.

'Yes,' Jess replied, turning her head towards him. 'I suppose it was in the charity shop when you came out with all that info about the helmet.'

Josh lay back on his bed and stared thoughtfully at the ceiling. 'Well, to tell the truth, even before that I got a really weird feeling when I saw the poppies in the school car park. In fact, those blood-red flowers have been giving me goose bumps ever since.'

'OK,' Jess said, turning back to the desk. '1...Poppies

71

in school car park. 2...Info on World War 1 helmet mysteriously coming into your head. What's next?'

Josh stared at the ceiling. 'Hmm...yes...the smell of pipe tobacco in Miss Robinson's office. In fact, I've picked up the smell a few times. That *really* gives me the creeps.'

Jess scribbled frantically on the piece of paper. 'OK. I think I know what comes next. The war memorial and the woman in black standing in front of it.'

'OMG! Was that scary or what!' Josh said, a shiver running down his spine at the thought of it. 'We still don't know who *she* is.' He suddenly sat up. 'Hey... do you think the woman in black could have been Great-Great-Grandma?'

'Possibly,' Jess replied, still making rapid notes. 'And when we found the war memorial, *why* didn't it have Great-Great-Grandad's name on it?'

'This is getting so confusing,' Josh sighed, lying back down and staring at the ceiling again. 'It was deffo there when I saw it on my laptop.'

'OK. Don't worry. Just keep a clear head,' Jess instructed him. 'What was the next weird thing that happened?'

'The soldier in the poppies.'

Jess stopped scribbling and looked over at her brother. 'You've seen him twice, haven't you?'

Josh nodded solemnly. 'He waved at me the second time.'

'*Seriously* scary,' Jess said, returning to her notes.

'Well if you think that's scary, you should have been there when I was playing Front Line 1 on the computer and I got blasted off my seat.'

'You never told me about that?' Jess said, turning back to him with big eyes. 'What happened?'

Josh sat up again. 'I'm sure it had something to do with the helmet. I put it on, see, while I was playing the game. And then everything sort of got real.'

'Like you were really in the game?' Jess asked.

'Exactly. I could even smell burning. And when an enemy grenade landed close, it actually blasted me off my seat. Mum came up to see what had happened. I didn't tell her. She wouldn't have believed me anyway.'

'That helmet might be the key to this,' Jess suggested. 'Can I have another look at it?'

Josh nodded and retrieved it from under the bed. He passed it to his sister.

'And finally...the weirdest thing of all,' she said, peering into the underside of the helmet. 'S O P.'

Josh walked over and looked at the lettering inside the lining. 'You don't really believe this was Great-Great-Grandad's helmet, do you?'

Jess stared up at her brother. 'Stanley Oswald Palmer. It's got to be. That's why Grandad was so shocked.' She passed the helmet back to Josh, went back to the desk and sat down.

Josh put the helmet back under his bed. 'Are you writing that down?'

Jess shook her head. She held up the sheet of paper, tore it in half and then tore it in half again.

'What are you doing?' Josh asked with a sense of panic in his voice.

'No need for this. It's clear to me what's happening.'

Josh sat bolt upright on the end of his bed and looked

his sister straight in the face. 'Go on then...what?'

Jess stood up and made her way to the door. She turned and looked across at her brother. 'Great-Great-Grandfather Stanley. He's haunting you.'

Josh swallowed hard. 'But why me?'

'Because he needs to tell you something; that's what all this weird stuff is leading up to. I'm sure of it.'

'Sis...I'm scared,' Josh said with a tremor in his voice.

'Don't be,' Jess said reassuringly. 'He's not going to hurt you. And I'll be right beside you every step of the way.' And saying this, she left the room.

Josh's mind whirled. He felt sure that Jess was right. She was very clever and he knew that only too well.

She probably will make a great detective one day!

He took his time getting ready for bed and headed off downstairs to watch TV...to try and relax his mind a little.

But it was no good.

The drinking chocolate helped, but TV was boring compared to what was really happening in his life right now.

...Unsurprisingly, that night, Josh tossed and turned and barely slept a wink.

MISTS OF TIME

The next morning, during breakfast, Mr Palmer looked out of the kitchen window with concern. 'I'm glad I'm working from home today. Have you seen it out there? A real 'pea-souper'.'

The twins tucked into their breakfast cereal as Mrs Palmer joined her husband and peered out. 'Ugh...I hate fog.'

'Maybe we should stay at home, Mum,' Josh said hopefully. 'Fog's dangerous.'

'Nice try,' Mrs Palmer replied, half laughing. 'You might get away with a 'snow day' now and then, but so far I've never heard of 'fog days'.'

Josh glanced across the table at Jess and raised his eyebrows.

Mr Palmer smiled at his wife. 'Why don't I do the

school run this morning and give you a break?'

Mrs Palmer accepted the offer gratefully and a short while later her husband was driving the twins towards Pheasant Bank Academy. With headlights on full beam and fog lights doing their best, he steered the car carefully through the swirling mist.

'Did Mum tell you...?' Mr Palmer said, leaning forward and staring fixedly through the windscreen. '... Grandad rang. He's coming over on Saturday morning.'

'Really?' Jess replied. 'He doesn't usually visit...not since Gran died anyway. Maybe he just wants to see the new house.'

Mr Palmer nodded towards the windscreen, 'Maybe. Anyway he seemed really keen.'

Josh said nothing. But inwardly the news of Grandad's impending visit made him feel nervous. He glanced over his shoulder at Jess. She stared back at him with her 'knowing look'.

Mr Palmer eased the car through the school gates. 'Phew...made it. Take care getting out. You can hardly see your hand in front of your face.'

The twins thanked him and got out. Josh glanced straight over to the poppies, but the embankment was shrouded in thick fog. It was impossible to see anything.

'Why do you think Grandad's so keen to visit?' Josh asked his sister as they made their way towards the school entrance.

'I don't know, but I bet it's got something to do with why he was so upset when we went to see him.'

'Just what I was thinking,' Josh nodded.

The twins walked into school and made their way to

Viking Class. The school seemed quieter than usual and it soon became clear that a good number of pupils had been delayed by the thick fog. Miss Robinson cancelled the school assembly and sent a note around asking form tutors to delay starting lessons until more latecomers had arrived.

This suited Josh very much. It gave him a chance to work on some artwork he'd started for the school's World War 1 theme – a picture of a soldier standing amongst the poppies. He felt driven to finish it.

'That's looking *very* good, Josh. I love the attention to detail. Especially the accuracy of the soldier's uniform.'

Josh was so intent on his drawing, he didn't look behind. He knew it was his form tutor, Mr Schofield. 'Thank you, Sir.'

Mr Schofield leaned closer over Josh's shoulder, '... Though the poppy leaves aren't quite accurate,' he added. 'Why don't you take a look at your pressed flower?'

'I never finished mine, Sir,' Josh explained, finally looking up at his form tutor. 'I suppose I could ask Jess if I could take a look at hers.'

Mr Schofield stepped back and strode across to the classroom window. 'The fog's lifted a little. I can see more pupils arriving. Why don't you nip out into the car park, Josh, and bring a few poppy leaves back with you? You can study them up close and get the structure more accurate in your drawing.'

A fluttering feeling invaded Josh's stomach. He really did *not* want to go outside...but he'd no idea why! 'They're all a bit withered and faded now, Sir. But I could check them out in a book or on the internet.'

Mr Schofield fell strangely silent. He continued to gaze out of the window in the direction of the embankment.

'Are you all right, Sir?' Josh asked him.

He turned to Josh and stared across at him with a strange look in his eyes, 'I *definitely* think you should go outside and gather a few poppy leaves, Josh. There's nothing quite so good as the *real* thing.'

Josh gulped. Mr Schofield was staring at him like some sort of zombie. It was so unlike him.

'You'll need these,' Mr Schofield said, handing Josh a pair of scissors.

Josh took the scissors and made his way to the classroom door. Jess watched him with a worried look on her face.

'Take care, Josh, it's still murky out there,' Mr Schofield called after him.

A few minutes later, Josh was walking across the school car park towards the embankment. A few cars were still arriving. He avoided them carefully and walked on into the poppies.

...But the fog thickened again and shrouded everything.

Josh couldn't believe it. Not only could he not *see* anything...but everything fell deathly silent and not a single sound could be heard. He knelt on the ground and felt the poppy leaves, cold and clammy in his hand... eagerly trying to convince himself that he wasn't dreaming. His ears still straining, he cut one of the plants at the base of its stem and rose to his feet again.

'HELLO! IS ANYBODY THERE?' he called out, hoping that some parent or teacher would hear him and guide him back into school.

But still not a sound...and no one came!

He took a few steps towards where he thought the edge of the embankment was....BUMP! Something big and hard barred his way. He reached out to touch it – its surface felt ice-cold with sharp edges. As the fog thinned a little, Josh's eyes almost popped from their sockets. There, in front of him, stood what looked like a gravestone, formed in the shape of a marble cross. As he struggled to make sense of things, the fog suddenly lifted and the sun broke through, shining brightly from a brilliant blue sky filled with white fluffy clouds.

...And now Josh saw that he was completely surrounded by gravestones, countless marble crosses stretching in long lines in every direction as far as the eye could see. He realised at once that he was standing in some sort of war cemetery. Every gravestone shone out whiter than white, and the grass growing between them was a verdant green and immaculately manicured. At first, a warm glow spread through his body; it made him feel good to think that so many fallen heroes were remembered here with such compassion.

...And then a different thought entered his head. Beneath every cross was a DEAD hero. So many men killed in their prime...having given up their precious lives for their country.

Tears began to trickle down Josh's cheeks as the immense scale of the war cemetery mirrored the immense sense of loss.

Wiping his tears on his sleeve, he leaned forward and read the inscription on the grave he'd just bumped into:

PRIVATE HENRY JAMESON
South Lancashire Regiment
25th JULY 1916   AGE 18

Josh was shocked. He'd always thought of soldiers as fully-grown men. But this dead 'man' was only a boy... *aged 18*. His mind went to his favourite cousin, Jack. *He* was 18 and had only just finished his A-levels.

Underneath the inscription were some more words etched into the white stone:

WILL SOME KIND HAND
IN A FOREIGN LAND
PLACE A FLOWER
ON MY SON'S GRAVE

Before Josh had time to think or do anything else, the fog came down as quickly as it had lifted. He dropped to his knees, held onto the cold marble and with tears streaming down his cheeks placed his cut poppy on top of the grave.

'You're a good lad, Josh,' a voice from behind him said softly. 'Don't get too upset. It'll all be right in the end.'

Josh swung round and gasped at the sight of the soldier...standing tall in the swirling mist...a bayoneted rifle in one hand and a mud-splattered backpack in the other.

GRANDAD'S VISIT

Josh sat opposite his twin sister during lunch and hardly touched his food, despite the fact that it was chips, sausages and beans...his favourite.

'So, spill!' urged Jess, tucking in heartily to her own food. 'You looked like you'd just seen a ghost when you came back into class.'

'That's the point,' Josh said mysteriously. 'I *had* just seen a ghost...Great-Great- Grandad!'

Jess stopped chewing and stared across at him with her mouth full and her cheeks bulging.

'You look like a hamster!' Josh said without so much as a smile. 'Look...if I tell you exactly what happened, you'll think I'm crazy.'

Jess nodded. 'I already think you're crazy.' She began chewing again.

'...But I'm going to tell you anyway.'

Whilst Jess continued with her meal, Josh told her exactly the series of events that had taken place in the school car park. By the time he got to the bit where the ghostly soldier had appeared, Jess was staring at him spellbound.

'He told me all would be OK in the end,' Josh said quietly.

Jess swallowed and stared hard at her brother. 'Did he say anything else?'

'Yes. He said something about me being called up to the real Front Line 1.'

Jess reached for her dessert – treacle sponge with custard. 'It's funny he should mention your computer game. It's like he knew what was in your mind.'

'Just like you do sometimes,' Josh agreed.

'Maybe it's a family thing,' Jess suggested. 'Anyway... when is this next meeting with Great-Great-Grandad's ghost supposed to take place?'

Josh finally took a mouthful of food and shook his head. 'He didn't say. He just said, 'I'll see you soon, boy,' and disappeared.'

'Just as quickly as the fog did,' Jess added. 'I'll never forget the look on Mr Schofield's face when he spotted you kneeling on the embankment. It looked like you were praying.'

Josh felt himself begin to blush. It had been really embarrassing walking back into Viking Class with a handful of crushed poppy leaves and the knees of his trousers stained green.

...And yet Mr Schofield had not questioned him or

said anything. It was almost as if the form tutor had been in on it.

'Or under the control of somebody or something responsible for the whole spooky experience,' Jess had finally surmised.

Josh hadn't really understood what Jess had meant by that. That was just Jess being Jess...brighter than bright as usual.

*

The rest of the week passed without incident. Nothing untoward happened and Josh decided to stay well clear of Front Line 1 for the time being. The World War 1 helmet remained firmly under his bed. All Josh could think about was Grandad's forthcoming visit on Saturday morning.

...And now Saturday morning had arrived. And he and Jess kept taking it in turns to look out of the sitting room window to try and spot him.

'He's here! He's coming up the path. At last!' Josh yelled out.

Jess ran to the kitchen door to let him in.

'Slow down!' Mrs Palmer said firmly. 'Anybody would think the Queen's arrived.'

Jess let her grandfather in and took his coat. He was carrying a white plastic bag, which he held onto.

'Your new house took a bit of finding,' Grandad George said.

'Well it's great to see you, Grandad,' Jess said, leading him into the sitting room.

Josh was on the sofa beside his mother. Grandad

George seated himself in an armchair by the window and Jess sat cross-legged on the carpet.

Before anyone could say anything, Mr Palmer walked in. 'Hi, Dad...great to see you. Shall I put the kettle on?'

'Thought you'd never ask,' Grandad George said, half-smiling. 'I'm parched after the long journey. Seems like the other side of the world.'

'Well it's only the other side of the Pennines,' Mr Palmer laughed. 'Tea or coffee?'

Grandad George decided on tea and Mr Palmer retreated to the kitchen.

'So why the urgent phone call to come over?' Mrs Palmer asked.

Josh looked at Jess. She looked back at him.

'Just wanted to give your new place the once over,' Grandad George replied.

'Well it's always good to see you,' Mrs Palmer replied. 'And now that you've found us, we'll hope to see you a bit more often.'

'Is there anything else, Grandad?' Jess asked him directly. 'Dad said you sounded like it was a bit urgent on the phone.'

Grandad George smiled and shook his head. 'That girl of yours, Alice. She's as bright as a button and twice as quick as a whippet!'

Mr Palmer re-entered the room with a mug of steaming tea. They all watched as Grandad George delved into his white plastic bag and brought out a rectangular tin.

'There's no need to bring your own biscuits, Dad,' Mr Palmer laughed. 'We've plenty of our own in the kitchen.'

Grandad George smiled faintly. 'Jess is right – as usual – there was another reason I was so keen to get over to see you...to give this to Josh.'

Josh's mouth fell open as his grandad handed him the tin.

'What's in it?' Josh asked.

'Well there's only one way to find out,' Grandad George replied, nodding towards the tin lid.

Everyone watched with bated breath as Josh pulled at the lid. It was tight and Josh guessed it hadn't been open for some time, but it finally came off with a clang and fell onto the carpet.

'Wow...medals!' Josh gasped, peering into the tin. 'War medals.' He took the two gleaming medals from the tin and caressed them in his fingers.

Grandad George spoke with real sadness in his voice, 'I'm sorry I was a bit abrupt when you asked me about your great-great-grandad Stanley and the First World War. It's just that things aren't always what they seem.'

'But why, George?' Mrs Palmer asked, sipping her tea. 'Surely if he won medals, you'd be proud.'

'Exactly!' Mr Palmer agreed. '*Anyone* would be proud.'

Whilst Josh and Jess examined the medals, Grandad George took a sip of tea. 'Like I said, things aren't always what they seem. Those medals aren't the only things my grandad left behind when he died. I was only seven years old when Grandma died. Me and Dad found some interesting things in a trunk in her loft. The tin was one of them.'

'Why...what else did you find?' Mrs Palmer asked.

'We found his army boots, his rifle...and this!'

They all watched as he delved back into the plastic bag and came out with a large brown envelope. It looked old...but important. It had some sort of official stamp on it.

Mrs Palmer looked taken aback. 'What is it?'

Grandad George nodded solemnly. 'Court-martial papers.'

Mr Palmer nearly dropped his drink. 'I don't understand.'

Josh and Jess looked across at Grandad George's sad features, awaiting his reply.

'Desertion! He won his medals and then lost his nerve. It was in France, during his last active service. When the order came to charge, they say he turned and ran away from the enemy. He was found later by his commanding officer...and...and...I don't like to say what happened next. Let's just say that Grandad didn't survive and these court-martial papers were sent on to Grandma Betty after his death.'

Mr Palmer looked dismayed. 'You've kept this to yourself all this time.'

'I know. I'm sorry,' Grandad George sighed. 'It was wrong of me. You're all family and you've got every right to know. When young Josh turned up with Grandad's helmet...well, that spooked me good and proper.'

They all sipped their drinks quietly. It was Jess who finally broke the silence:

'Well I think that no one's got the right to judge that man,' she said sharply. 'Nobody knows how they'd react in something as horrible as war...all that killing and suffering. Who knows what poor old Great-Great-Grandad Stanley was thinking?'

At Jess's words the room fell silent again. Grandad George looked straight across at his granddaughter. He said nothing...but his eyes filled with tears.

GLOOM AND DOOM

It was Sunday morning and the Palmer house was very quiet.

Since Grandad George's visit the day before, a cloud of gloom had hung over everything. No one had spoken much and it seemed to Josh that he, Jess, Mum and Dad were keeping pretty much to themselves.

Mr Palmer was giving the car its weekly wash. He usually whistled loudly while doing it...but not this morning! He worked in silence and looked thoughtful.

Mrs Palmer was ironing – a job she never did on Sunday mornings – but she worked on the pile of clean washing as though her life depended on it. She didn't even switch the radio on to listen to her favourite weekend request show!

Josh was in his room lying on his bed, holding the war

medals up and staring at the vivid colours of the ribbons. He wanted to feel proud of them...but he couldn't!

Jess had retired to her room after breakfast too. She'd said something about being behind with her homework. Josh knew that was a lie...she *never* got behind with her homework!

Josh went across to his sister's room.

KNOCK...KNOCK, KNOCK.

'What do you want?' Jess called out to her brother.

'Just wanted a chat.'

'Come in.'

Josh opened the door and saw his sister sitting on the end of her bed. She was holding a box of tissues on her lap and wiping her eyes.

'You've been crying!' he said full of surprise.

'Very observant, little brother!' Jess replied sarcastically.

Josh sat at his sister's desk and looked across at her. He spoke softly. 'I'm guessing you're upset about Great-Great-Grandad Stanley being a deserter.'

Jess nodded solemnly. 'And I feel really upset for Grandad George. You could see the hurt in his eyes. He looked so ashamed.'

'It's affected us all. Mum and Dad are acting most subdued.'

Jess nodded again. 'They're ashamed, too.'

Josh walked over to his sister, sat by her on the end of the bed and put his arm around her shoulder. 'But *you* were right, Sis. Nobody really knows what it was like fighting in that war. Maybe after winning those two bravery medals he lost his nerve and went crazy!'

Jess wiped her eyes again, turned to her brother and

looked serious. 'Maybe that's why he's haunting you. Maybe he wants to tell you *why* he lost his nerve, Josh. Maybe he just wants to explain everything.'

Josh felt his heart begin to race. Jess had just given him lots of 'maybes', but the biggest 'maybe' of all was that *maybe* she was right!

*

After a very quiet morning, the Palmer family went into town. It was a pleasant afternoon, the weakened autumnal sun doing its best to brighten up the old market town, whilst the bells of Rossfield's St Nicholas's church resounded cheerfully through the crisp, clear air.

Having shared a coffee together, the Palmers strolled along the Rossfield Canal and the sight of brightly-coloured narrow boats lined up along the towpath improved everyone's mood.

No one mentioned Grandad's visit or spoke of the Great War!

'Rossfield is a very attractive town,' Mrs Palmer remarked cheerfully. 'I'm glad we moved here. I think we're really going to like it.'

Mr Palmer nodded in agreement. 'And the job's going well. It was a good move.'

Josh and Jess said nothing. They both knew what each other was thinking.

Rossfield may be a pleasant town, but they still missed their friends.

Heading back down the canal towpath, the impressive spire of the church loomed before them.

'Can we just take a peek inside?' Mrs Palmer asked. 'I love old churches.'

No one objected and a short while later the four of them were inside the old church. The ancient building was completely empty, the air cold, a heavy silence hanging over everything.

'I'd like to light a candle for Great-Great-Grandad Stanley,' Jess suddenly said loudly. Her voice echoed eerily around the church.

Mr Palmer bit his lip and said nothing.

Mrs Palmer put her arm around Jess and nodded in agreement. Josh shrugged his shoulders. He was at a loss what to say.

Whilst Mum and Jess walked over to the little row of candles, Josh made his way to the other side of the church to explore a small chapel to the right of the main altar. The chapel was a dark and gloomy space with its own altar at its centre and a huge marble plaque on the wall above it. The plaque was adorned with some sort of coat of arms and bordered with Gothic images of skulls and bones. It gave Josh the creeps, but he felt drawn to move closer and read the words etched onto the plaque's surface:

In memory of the 24 brave young men
of the Rossfield Light Infantry Regiment
who lost their lives during
The Great War at The Battle of
The Somme 1916:
May their souls rest in eternal peace.

As Josh took in the words and glanced around, it dawned on him that this was a remembrance chapel, dedicated to the people of Rossfield who had fallen in the war. A stained glass window on the right showed war scenes on each of its panels, whilst a plaque mounted on the wall beside it was dedicated to those who had served in the Red Cross.

...But it was the tomb standing against the wall on his left that drew Josh in more than anything. The marble tomb was rectangular, about the size of a coffin, with a full-size marble soldier in uniform lying submissively across its surface. The soldier's eyes gazed sightlessly into space, a rifle clutched across his chest and an inscription carved into the stone at his feet.

Whoahh...that is seriously spooky!

Josh crept nearer so he could read the inscription:

Truth is all-important.
We live by it, fight for it and die by it.

'JOSH...COME ON! WE'RE GOING!'

Josh turned and saw his dad standing by the entrance calling out to him. Mum and Jess had already gone out.

'OK, Dad. Coming!' Josh called back. The thought of getting outside and back into the bright sunshine appealed to him. The little remembrance chapel had made him feel gloomy again. He watched as Dad disappeared outside so that he was the only one left in the church. A creepy feeling suddenly came over him.

He headed quickly for the door but felt compelled to look back over his shoulder towards the chapel.

He screamed inwardly as goose bumps spread through his body and a chill rattled down his spine.

...The stone soldier was moving...hunching itself up on to its elbows and waving a cold, marble arm towards him.

*

Josh lay in bed going over and over the afternoon's events. Since returning home he and Jess had had another 'secret meeting' and Josh had told his sister what had happened in the church.

He'd even remembered the words etched onto the soldier's tomb. For some reason they had stuck in his mind:

Truth is all-important. We live by it, fight for it and die by it.

Jess had listened intently, made more notes and promised Josh she would get her head around it. She felt sure that the spooky event in the church was yet another piece in the jigsaw.

It took a long time for Josh to get off to sleep. It was hardly surprising...his mind was full of swirling images and confusing thoughts. And moving stone statues were the stuff of nightmares!

Some time in the early hours he awoke and found himself sitting at his desk, looking down at the artwork he'd started at school. But the World War 1 soldier no longer stood in a field of poppies. Instead of being surrounded by masses of crimson flowers, the soldier was now standing in a desolate and depressing landscape...

dead trees and coils of barbed wire scattered over barren, muddy ground.

In the bottom right hand corner of the drawing were the words: 'Western Front, The Somme, 1916,' written in black ink.

At first, Josh shook his head in disbelief, wondering who had tampered with his artwork. But as wakefulness dawned over him, he realised he was holding a pencil in one hand and a black pen in the other.

I've done this...but how? I've heard of sleepwalking, but I've never heard of 'sleepdrawing'!

He took the striking image back to bed with him, held it up to the light and studied it again. He looked at the words he'd written in the bottom right-hand corner and focused on the word 'Somme'; he'd seen that word somewhere but couldn't remember where.

He folded the drawing neatly and placed it under his pillow...and by some miracle managed to drop straight back to sleep.

BATTLES

Monday morning, Lesson 2. Josh sat at his desk with his 'sleepdrawing' picture in front of him, staring down at the writing in the bottom right-hand corner:

'Western Front, The Somme, 1916'

Mr Schofield walked into the classroom, went straight over to the whiteboard and wrote 'BATTLES OF WORLD WAR 1' at the top of the board.

'As part of our Great War theme, I thought it would be a good idea if we chose one of the more significant battles of the First World War and researched it. Then we can write about it and add it to our display boards. What do you think?'

The class nodded and murmured their approval. Josh looked across at Jess. She was nodding enthusiastically, too.

Mr Schofield continued: 'I'm going to put a list of well-known World War 1 battles on the board and then we'll make a decision which one to use.'

The class sat quietly as the teacher began putting the list up on the board:

1. The Marne

2. Gallipoli

3. Jutland

4. The Somme...

Josh almost fell off his chair. There was that word again, 'Somme'. *That's it!*

He remembered where he'd seen it previously – on the remembrance plaque above the altar in their local church.

Mr Schofield finished his list:

5. The Brusilov Offensive

6. Passchendaele

7. Ypres

A hand shot into the air, 'How can we decide which one to choose if we don't know anything about them, Sir?'

'That is the most sensible thing you've ever said, Millie.' Mr Schofield looked from her to the rest of the class. 'All of these battles are worthy of our time. I suggest we have a vote. Just choose the one that seems to attract your attention.'

Josh gulped. He knew immediately which one attracted *his* attention.

'Let's have a show of hands first,' Mr Schofield suggested. 'Maybe most of you will go for the same one and that will be 'problem solved'.'

'I don't think anyone should go for number six,' somebody called out. '...It's too tricky to spell!'

Everyone laughed and nodded in agreement.

'How about number one – The Battle of the Marne?' the teacher asked.

Almost every hand in Viking Class shot up.

Mr Schofield laughed. 'I'm guessing that's because it's the *easiest* one on the list to spell.'

He continued to read out the list, just a few hands going up for each one. When he got to number four – The Somme – Josh was the only one to put his hand up. Whether the class picked it or not, he was determined to find out more about it.

A few other hands went up as the rest of the list was read out. Josh noted that Jess put her hand up for number six. *Trust sis. She could spell anything,* Josh thought to himself.

'Well that's that then,' Mr Schofield said. 'It's quite clear which battle will be the subject of our research. The Battle of the Somme.'

'But...but...Sir!' someone near the front stammered.

'No arguments, Ryan!' Mr Schofield said firmly. 'It was a democratic vote and it didn't take much to see that almost everyone wanted number four.'

Whilst Mr Schofield turned back to the whiteboard, everyone in the class muttered in disbelief. Josh couldn't believe it! He looked over to Jess and she gave him a strange look. He turned back towards the front and saw that Mr Schofield had rubbed out the list and written on the board:

THE BATTLE OF THE SOMME

...And then the teacher turned and looked over at Josh...and Josh saw that Mr Schofield had that strange look in his eyes again – the same bewitched look he'd had when he'd sent Josh out in the fog to get a poppy.

Josh felt his heart begin to beat faster and quickly looked away.

Somme...Somme....Somme. It seemed that the word was haunting him...just like Great-Great-Grandad Stanley. There was obviously some connection between them.

*

After the strange lesson with Mr Schofield, Josh couldn't wait to get home to do some research into the Battle of the Somme and he was sure Jess would feel the same way.

All that Mr Schofield had told them so far was that it took place in 1916 in Northern France on the Western Front, and that it had been one of the bloodiest battles in history.

At 7 pm that evening, after Josh had spent a good hour researching on the internet, he made his way to Jess's room:

KNOCK...KNOCK, KNOCK.

'ENTER!'

Josh went in and found Jess sitting at her desk scanning over a piece of paper. 'Guessed you'd be hard at it,' he said seriously. 'I bet you know everything there is to know about the Somme battle. After that business at school, it's looking like Great-Great-Grandad Stanley did, too. He *must* have fought in it.'

Jess looked up at him and smiled. 'I agree...but I knew *you'd* get on with all of that. I've been putting the *whole* jigsaw thing together.'

'Playing detective again!' Josh replied. He sat heavily on the end of his sister's bed. A nervous flutter formed in his stomach. 'So, what do you reckon?'

Jess rose to her feet and held the piece of paper out in front of her. 'This is what I reckon. Great-Great-Grandad Stanley is haunting you because he wants to tell you what really happened to him in the war...and like you say... probably at the Battle of the Somme.'

'What do you mean?'

'What I mean is that I don't think he was a deserter... least of all a coward.'

Josh nodded. 'You're right. No way would a coward win two war medals.'

'Exactly!' Jess agreed. 'I think he wants *you* to know the truth.'

Josh's mind flashed back to the words he'd seen in the church:

'Truth is all-important. We live by it, fight for it and die by it.'

'OMG! I think you're right, Sis. The soldier's tomb in the church. Those words were carved into the stone by his feet.'

'And you reckon you saw the statue move...*terrifying*. But I think it confirms that whatever you saw or didn't see, someone was trying to tell you something. And we all know who that 'someone' is,' Jess said with a serious tone in her voice.

' Great-Great-Grandad Stanley!' Josh said, biting into his bottom lip.

'I reckon you should ring Grandad George,' Jess said,

placing the sheet of paper back on the desk.

'Why?'

'...To ask him exactly what happened to Great-Great-Grandad Stanley.'

Josh looked across at his sister with sad eyes. 'But he didn't want to tell us. He might be upset if I ask him.'

'Tell him we're doing a research project on the First World War at school. Ask him if he knows which the last battle was that Great-Great-Grandad Stanley fought in and see if he'll tell you exactly what they think happened to him.'

Josh scratched his forehead. 'Hmmm. Because what they *think* happened might not be true.'

'You're getting the idea, Bro,' Jess said excitedly. 'And if we ring when Mum and Dad aren't around, I think he might tell you.'

'Well if I remember, he did say we've a right to know,' Josh added.

'Anyway...what did you find out about the Battle of the Somme?' Jess asked, sitting on the bed by his side.

Now it was Josh's turn to read from his sheet of paper:

'Well...it lasted 141 days, from 1st July 1916 to 18th November in the same year.'

'Wow! That's some battle,' Jess sighed.

'It took place on the banks of the Somme river in Northern France.'

'And it was the British against the Germans, I suppose,' Jess said.

'Not exactly! It was the British Empire actually. And the French joined with them against the Germans.'

'If it was the British Empire, then the Canadians and

the Australians must have been involved.'

Josh looked at his sister. 'You're so clever. They were known as the 'Allies'.'

Jess nodded. 'So the Allies against the Germans...what else did you find out?'

Josh paused for breath. 'Day 1 of the battle was the bloodiest day in British military history. Nearly 20,000 British soldiers died.'

'What? In just one day?' Jess exclaimed.

'There's worse...' Josh went on. 'In total there were over 1.3 million casualties.'

Jess rose slowly to her feet and clenched her fists. 'How can anyone justify all that killing?'

Josh looked down at his research findings again. 'And...the weather didn't help...it rained and rained, so the battlefield became a mud bath.'

'Who won?'

'Some would say the British won...or at least the Allies. But guess what... throughout the entire battle the Germans were only pushed back seven miles.'

'Unbelievable! What a waste of human life!' Jess said sadly.

'You're right. In fact loads of people have said it was one of the blackest times in human history.'

'Like I keep saying...' Jess went on. '...No one really knows what those soldiers must have been thinking. They were going through hell!'

Josh put his paper down and stared into space. 'And guess what else...when those guys were charging towards the enemy, they had to carry around 30 kilograms of gear on their backs.' He fell silent, refocused and glanced at

Jess. She was looking at him in a strange way.

'That wasn't on your list, was it? Where did you find that out?' Jess asked him.

Josh gulped. 'No idea! It just came into my head!' He quickly changed the subject. 'When should I ring Grandad?'

'Tomorrow lunchtime...at school. We'll get permission from Mr Schofield. We'll tell him we need to give Grandad a quick ring to get some info on the war theme. He's sure to let us ring from the school office.'

Josh gulped again. 'OK, Sis. Sounds like a plan,' he said confidently. But inwardly he felt nervous.

He couldn't begin to guess what was *supposed* to have happened to Great-Great-Grandad Stanley, and even more so what had *really* happened. But one thing was sure in Josh's mind....

...One way or another he was going to find out!

UPSETTING NEWS

Tuesday morning was windy, cold and dismal. As Mrs Palmer eased the car through the school gates, Josh glanced over at the poppies. The once blood-red blooms had faded further to pale pink and were swaying wildly in a strong northerly wind; it was almost as if they knew they were dying...waving a final farewell.

During morning lessons Josh found it hard to concentrate; he kept thinking about the phone call to Grandad George that he and Jess had planned for lunchtime. It was during History with Mr Schofield that Jess saw her chance.

'I'm hoping that you've succeeded in finding some information on The Battle of the Somme,' Mr Schofield said to the class. 'How about you, Ryan?'

'No problem, Sir,' Ryan replied cheerily. 'There's loads

of info on the internet.'

'And it seems that our great-great-grandad fought in the actual battle, Sir,' Jess blurted out.

Josh noted that the rest of the class looked impressed.

'That's great,' Mr Schofield said. 'How did you find out?'

'Grandad told us, Sir.'

'Of course,' Mr Schofield smiled. 'Did he have any other information about your great-great-grandad?'

'Well, it's funny you should say that, Sir,' Jess replied confidently. '...He was going to get some info together for us...which regiment he was in and all that sort of stuff. Is it OK if I ring him at lunchtime to see how he's getting on?'

Mr Schofield smiled again. 'No problem at all. I'm sure we'd all like to know. I'll get permission from the office for you to make the call.'

Josh felt guilty. And by the look on Jess's face he knew that she felt guilty too. Both he and his sister hated lying, but surely this was only one of those 'little white lies' that would help them make progress with their investigation.

*OK, Sis...*Josh thought to himself. *You've done well... let's see what Grandad has to say!*

*

Jess was told to report to the office after she'd had lunch. She arrived with Josh and the receptionist behind the glass panel, Mrs Moore, looked up at them and gestured for them to come through.

'OK, you two. Give me the number and I'll ring

through and get your Grandad for you.'

Josh felt his heart begin to flutter as Jess recited the number.

Mrs Moore rang it and waited. 'Hello. Is that Mr Palmer? I've got your lovely grandchildren in front of me. Is it OK if they have a word? Fine...I'll put Jess on.'

Jess took the phone. Mrs Moore got up and moved into an adjoining room.

Great...we're on our own, Josh thought to himself.

'Oh, hi, Grandad,' Jess began. 'We're ringing from school because I need to ask you something to do with the theme that we're working on...The Great War.'

There was a pause. Jess looked at Josh. She held her hand over the mouthpiece and whispered, 'He's gone quiet!'

She spoke into the phone again. 'Grandad...are you still there? Oh...yes...I know you said he was a deserter and all that, but we're actually doing some work on why some people became deserters. And, by the way, do you happen to know which regiment he was in? ...Manchester Light Infantry Regiment. That's great.' She reached out for the notepad and pencil on the receptionist's desk and scribbled the information down.

'If it doesn't upset you too much, Grandad, could you tell us exactly what happened to him?' She looked at Josh with big eyes as she waited for the response.

'I know it's upsetting...but like you said when you came to see us...we're all family and we ought to know... we're not kids anymore.'

Josh waited with bated breath as his sister listened for a response.

'Grandad...are you still there?' She looked at Josh and frowned. 'This is hopeless...I don't think he's going to tell us,' she whispered.

'Here...give it to me!' Josh said, taking the phone from her.

'Hi, Grandad. It's Josh. We're not putting the phone down 'til you tell us. Deserters used to be shot...executed... didn't they? Is that what happened to Great-Great-Grandad? You can tell us and I promise we won't be too upset or anything.' Now it was Josh's turn to stare at Jess as *he* waited for a response. He shook his head. 'Nothing!'

He spoke into the phone again. 'Look, Grandad, it's not like we knew him. It all happened way before we were even born.' He waited again.

'OK. Yes...I'm sitting down. Go on...' he raised a thumb to his sister and sat in the receptionist's chair.

*

'OK, Josh!' his grandad said slowly. 'I'll tell you what happened, but you have to be a man about it. No tears or anything like that. As you quite rightly said, it all happened a long time ago, and as that bright sister of yours just reminded me...you've every right to know.'

*

At the end of the phone call, Josh replaced the receiver, rose to his feet and felt his legs begin to wobble.

'OMG,' Jess exclaimed. 'Is it *really* that bad?'

Josh nodded solemnly. 'Yep!'

The receptionist re-entered the room. 'All OK?' She asked cheerily.

Josh forced a smile. 'Yes, thanks.'

'Hope you don't mind, but we made a few notes,' Jess said, pointing to the notepad.

Mrs Moore smiled, tore off the top page and handed it to Jess without looking at it. 'No problem at all,' she said kindly.

The twins left in silence. Josh felt a little faint, his mind still reeling from what Grandad George had told him.

As they headed down the busy main corridor, it was Jess who spoke first.

'I'm guessing by the look on your face that Great-Great-Grandad *was* executed? Did they shoot him?'

'Worse!' Josh replied, staring ahead into space.

'How can anything be worse than being shot?'

Josh stopped. As the school bell rang and everyone headed off to afternoon lessons, he turned and looked straight into his sister's worried face. 'It depends who did the shooting,' he said seriously. 'Do you want to know now or would you rather wait until after school?'

'Sorry, Josh, but I need to know now. We need to stick together on this. If it's upsetting you, then I should be upset too. So spill!'

Josh took a deep breath. 'OK...you're right. Great-Great-Grandad *was* shot for being a deserter. And it *did* happen at the Battle of the Somme.' He gulped and took another deep breath.

'*...He was shot in the back by his commanding officer.*'

107

MIXED FEELINGS

Josh found it hard to concentrate on afternoon lessons to say the least! And every time he looked over at his sister, she was either looking into space or staring down at her desk. It was easy to see that she was upset. In fact Mr Sylvester, the Maths teacher, had asked Jess if she was OK. Jess had nodded solemnly and said nothing.

By the time they got home Josh was confused by his feelings – upset and angry at the same time. Both he and Jess went straight up to their rooms, neither saying anything to their parents about the phone call to Grandad George.

As soon as Josh got into his room, he went straight over to his desk, picked up his computer game, Front Line 1, and threw it straight into his waste bin. He dived heavily onto his bed, flipped over and stretched back with his hands behind his head.

He stared up at the ceiling and went over and over the phone call to Grandad George. It was so hard to come to terms with.

It was bad enough that Great-Great-Grandad was a deserter, but still so unfair and unbelievable that he died in the way he did! As Jess had said, no one should judge anyone going through what those brave men who fought in the war had gone through. And that's why his sister was so upset; she would have forgiven Great-Great-Grandad Stanley for anything...including being a deserter!

But the idea of his commanding officer shooting him in the back...well, that was totally unbelievable!

Josh got off his bed and went over to his desk. He looked down and saw the drawing he'd done of the soldier on the battle front. The detail and accuracy were amazing. He still found it hard to believe that *he'd* drawn it and especially the way he'd finished it during his 'sleepdrawing' episode!

He sat down at his desk, took a rubber from his pencil case and rubbed out what he'd written in the bottom right-hand corner – 'Western Front, The Somme, 1916.'

Instead, he wrote along the bottom:

'Stanley Palmer – Manchester Light Infantry Regiment – Deserted during the Battle of the Somme, 1916.'

He was tempted to add that he'd been shot in the back by his commanding officer, but he thought better of it.

Tomorrow, he would hand it in at school to Mr Schofield and ask him to put it up on the display boards. He knew the teacher would be shocked, but he and everyone else had a right to know.

Whether anyone liked it or not, Great-Great-Grandad Stanley *was* a deserter.

As this thought went through Josh's head, he banged his fist down on his desk with such force that a glass of raspberry juice left from the night before toppled over on its side.

The juice ran everywhere. *It made Josh think of the enormous amount of blood spilt during the conflict of the Great War!*

*

That night it took Josh a long time to fall asleep. And when he did, he began to dream.

He dreamt that he'd got out of bed, wandered over to the waste bin and taken out the discarded computer game. Loading it into his PC, he readied himself for action... feeling angry and determined at the same time.

With great skill he quickly reached the enemy machine-gun post. As usual, he took out the gunner with a deadly accurate throw of a grenade and advanced towards the enemy trench. But this time he knew what was coming...*gas attack!*

He snatched up a gas mask from a dead soldier lying close by and continued to charge. As the siren sounded the arrival of the deadly gas, he continued towards the trench and reached it.

...And then...instead of controlling his avatar within his dream, he found he *was* the little figure, scrambling to the top of the trench's sloping side and peering over into the deep ditch.

The first things Josh saw were dead bodies, clothed in German uniform, littering the bottom of the trench and surrounded by discarded equipment. It was easy to see that the trench had been home to them for some considerable time. There was makeshift shelving containing metal mugs, cans and bottles, and a rough piece of wood panelling leant against another part of the trench with a cracked mirror at head height. Below the mirror was a shelf leaning at 45 degrees, its contents scattered in the mud beneath it...mugs, razors, hair brushes and other familiar everyday items.

The sight of the soldiers' day-to-day equipment brought a lump to Josh's throat...the Germans *were* the enemy, but they *were* also human...just like everyone else!

As Josh prepared to move on, to finally discover what lay beyond the front line, a sound reached his ears from the bottom of the trench.

'MIR HELFEN! MIR HELFEN!'

Josh saw that one of the 'dead bodies' in the bottom of the trench was still alive. The German called out to him again. 'KÖNNEN SIE MIR HELFEN?'

Josh found himself facing a real dilemma. Though he didn't speak a word of German, he knew by the sound of the soldier's cries that he was desperate for help. Should he descend down into the trench to help the wounded German...or leave him and advance onwards to find out what Level 4 had to offer?

BANG!

He felt a searing pain in his back...the screen went black. GAME OVER!

Josh woke up in a cold sweat. He sat up and felt round to his back...no pain...nothing! He lay down again and took a deep breath.

Phew! Dream over!

*

Over breakfast the next morning, he and Jess spoke in quiet whispers. He told Jess of his vivid dream. 'In fact, it was so real, when I got up, I went straight over to the waste bin to see if the computer game was still dumped inside it.'

'And was it?'

Josh nodded. 'I checked my back again in the mirror too. I know it sounds crazy, but I really did feel a horrible pain.'

Jess balanced a spoonful of breakfast cereal close to her lips and looked thoughtful, '...Like you'd been shot?'

Josh nodded again.

Jess gave him a sympathetic look. 'It must be tough for you to know what's real and what's not. There's some really weird stuff going on at the moment.' She looked over to Mum standing by the sink, just to make sure she wasn't listening, and leaned closer to Josh. 'I didn't sleep well myself. I just kept thinking about poor old Great-Great-Grandad Stanley.'

'Me, too!' Josh chipped in.

'It just doesn't add up,' Jess went on in low whispers. 'Two war medals and then shot in the back for being a coward. It's like we said before...something's not right.'

'Well it's not like we can do anything, can we?'

Jess looked him straight in the eye. 'Yes...we can wait.'

Josh gave his sister a puzzled look. 'What do you mean?'

'I still think that Great-Great-Grandad Stanley is trying to guide us towards the truth of what really happened. And don't forget the last thing he said to you.'

'He'll see me again soon,' Josh recalled.

'You're very quiet back there,' Mum suddenly called over her shoulder. 'Everything OK?'

'Fine, Mum!' the twins replied in perfect unison.

Jess spoke in low whispers again. 'Don't forget, whatever happens, I'll be with you all the way.'

Josh took in his sister's resolved expression.

Thank God I've got Jess on my side!

'So you think we should just wait?' he asked, going back to his breakfast cereal.

'I've never been so sure of anything, Bro. Something's going to happen very soon. I can sense it.' And saying this, Jess pushed a final spoonful of cereal into her mouth, slurped the last of her drink to wash it down, leant back in her chair and did the loudest burp Josh had ever heard.

As Mrs Palmer had a go at Jess for being so rude, Josh laughed until the tears streamed down his cheeks. The incident was just what he needed to break the tension.

...But as they left the breakfast table and readied themselves for school, Jess's words sank in. The truth was that Josh *had* sensed it, too...that something *was* going to happen...and sooner rather than later!

MESSAGES

Josh took his drawing of Great-Great-Grandad Stanley (deserter) to school, ready to hand in to Mr Schofield during Lesson 3, but by the time he and Jess had arrived, he'd changed his mind. If Jess was right and the truth was still to come out, then maybe it would be best to hang on to the drawing and keep it in his desk.

Just before Mr Schofield arrived for Lesson 3, Josh took it from his desk to have another look at it. His eyes went straight to what he'd written in the bottom right-hand corner:

'Stanley Palmer – Manchester Light Infantry Regiment – Deserted during the Battle of the Somme, 1916.'

He started thinking about handing it in again – maybe after getting rid of the deserter reference – when

Mr Schofield made his entrance. He looked straight at Jess. 'Did you manage to make your call, Jess?'

Jess nodded. 'Yes, Sir. He was in the Manchester Light Infantry Regiment.'

'Did you find out anything else about him?'

'He died in the Battle of the Somme, Sir.'

'That's a shame, Jess. So many brave men died in action. Every single one of them was a real hero.' He turned to the whiteboard. 'This morning we are going to discuss thousands of other men who fought in the Great War who were *not* labelled as heroes.'

The class watched in silence as Mr Schofield wrote on the smartboard in big, bold letters:

DESERTERS

Josh almost fell off his chair. He looked across to Jess and saw the stunned expression on her face.

'Who can tell me what we mean by a 'deserter'?' the teacher asked.

A number of hands went up.

'Yes, Millie?'

'Well, Sir...it's someone who runs off.'

'Sort of, Millie. But *who* runs off and *why*?'

Josh put his hand up.

'Yes, Josh?'

'It could be a soldier on either side, Sir. They lose their nerve and instead of charging forward...like they're supposed to...they run back...away from the action.'

'Like a coward, Sir,' Millie added.

'So who thinks that deserters in the Great War were cowards?' Mr Schofield asked.

Almost every hand went up, apart from Josh and Jess.

'Why isn't your hand up, Jess? What do you think about deserters?'

'Wars are so horrible, Sir. I don't think we should judge those who had to fight in them. Nobody knows how much they really suffered and what was going through their minds.'

Mr Schofield clapped his hands together. 'I absolutely agree with you, Jess. You have an old head on your young shoulders!' He turned and wrote again on the smartboard: SHELL SHOCK

'Anybody know what that means? Yes, Ryan?'

'It's when bombs and things go off. The loud blasts and other stuff affect the soldiers' nerves and make them go crazy.'

'That's about right, Ryan. Well done! Some of the soldiers lost their hearing, but many of them were more affected by their nerves. They couldn't stop shaking and were prone to panic attacks, even when they were home on leave, well away from the battlefield.'

A girl called Sophie spoke up. 'That's awful, Sir!'

'Some soldiers home on leave were so ill with shell shock that they didn't go back to battle when they were summoned. They were labelled 'deserters' too.'

'And what happened to them?' someone called out.

'They were executed,' Josh called back.

'It's disgusting! They shouldn't have been,' Jess called out after him.

'Who agrees with Jess?' Mr Schofield asked the class.

Every hand went up except one. It was the boy who always looked half-asleep and disinterested. 'I'd shoot every one of them,' he said. 'Complete cowards if you ask me.'

'Well, we didn't ask you!' Jess snapped at him. 'Those men fought to keep everyone safe...and that includes you.'

'But that's the point, deserters *didn't* fight. They were cowards. In any case...who cares?' The boy shrugged his shoulders.

'Hmmm....I can see emotions are running high. That's good. We all have a right to express our view.' The teacher smiled across at Jess. 'I happen to think you're right, Jess. We should never judge anyone...we will never really understand what those men had to go through.'

Josh turned in his seat and glowered at the boy behind. 'Some deserters had already fought in horrific battles and even won medals before their nerve went. And some of us *do* care. If it hadn't been for them, we might not be here now!'

'Well said, Bro!' Jess called out loudly.

'Yeah...well said,' some of the others called out in agreement.

The boy behind Josh just shrugged his shoulders again. 'Yeah...yeah...whatever!'

Josh felt the adrenalin beginning to course through his veins. On a sudden impulse, he reached inside his desk and pulled out the 'deserter' picture.

'Speaking of deserters, Sir, would you mind putting this up in our display? I finished it at home. You know... the soldier.'

'Oh, I know the one. Amazing attention to detail. Thank you, Josh.' He walked over and took it from him. 'But what has it got to do with deserters?'

'Look at the writing, Sir. Bottom right-hand corner.'

The class watched in silence as the teacher examined it.

He glanced back at Josh with a puzzled expression. 'Like I said, Josh, what's it got to do with deserters? And why did you put tomorrow's date on it?'

He passed it back to Josh. Josh looked straight to the bottom right-hand corner and read the writing:

'Stanley Palmer – Manchester Light Infantry Regiment – The Battle of the Somme, 15th October, 2019.'

'Sorry, Sir...I don't know...I'm not sure....' Josh stammered.

'It's OK, Josh. I'd like to say you must have had a 'senior moment', but you're far too young.'

Josh wasn't sure what Mr Schofield meant, but one thing he did know...there was no way *he'd* got rid of the deserter reference and definitely no way *he'd* written tomorrow's date.

This was deffo another weird happening. A message maybe...from Great-Great-Grandad Stanley?

He turned and looked across to Jess. She was nodding... reading his mind and agreeing. And then he sensed what she was thinking. It *was* a message from Great- Great-Grandad...that something *was* about to happen soon...in fact *very* soon...on the 15th October, 2019.

...*Tomorrow!*

WAR CALLING

After the strange incidents in Lesson 3, Josh spent the rest of the day in a daze. Everything seemed so surreal. By the look on Jess's face, she was feeling exactly the same.

At the end of school, when Mrs Palmer arrived to collect them, the twins climbed into the car in silence.

'You two look very sheepish,' Mrs Palmer said, driving slowly away. '...And it's hardly surprising!'

Josh glanced over his shoulder to the back seat. Jess shrugged her shoulders and looked back at him with her *'I've really no idea what she's on about'* expression.

Mrs Palmer glanced in the rear mirror and saw Jess's face. 'Don't look like that! Grandad George has been on the phone.'

Josh stared forward in silence. Jess did the same.

'...And you both know why,' Mrs Palmer continued.

'You've no right phoning your grandad behind my and Dad's back.'

'What did he say?' Jess asked, trying to sound calm.

Josh tensed. He guessed what was coming next.

'He told us how you'd put pressure on him to tell you what happened to Great- Great-Grandad Stanley. He'd already told you that he didn't want to talk about it...but you had to go on at him, didn't you? I'm very disappointed.'

More silence from the twins.

'He's upset because he gave way and told you what happened. And now he thinks *you're* upset and it's his fault!'

'But we're *not* upset, Mum,' Josh said firmly.

'No, Josh!' Jess interrupted. 'We *are* upset, but only because now we know what really happened to him. We needed to know. We're not kids!'

'That's just the point. You *are* kids. You're not even teenagers yet. You take too much on yourselves! Your dad and I are adults and even we were sickened when we found out how Great-Great-Grandad Stanley died.'

'Sorry, Mum,' Josh said softly, guessing that Mum's rant was almost over.

'Sorry, Mum,' Jess added.

'OK,' Mrs Palmer said quietly. 'We'll say no more about it. But I don't want to hear any more talk on The Great War for the foreseeable.'

The twins nodded silently.

...But the thought going through Josh's head was that if Mum wasn't going to hear anything more about The Great War...*he* most certainly was!

The next morning, as Josh sat down to breakfast, he felt extremely nervous and *very* tired. He'd hardly slept a wink, thinking and worrying about Great-Great-Grandad's ominous message. He saw Dad's newspaper on the table beside him. He looked straight to the top of the front page to check the date: 15th October, 2019.

*So I guess this is it...*Josh thought to himself...*today's the day!*

Jess arrived and pulled up a chair beside him. 'Anything happened yet?' she whispered.

Josh shook his head and frowned. 'Come on...we've only just got up!'

Mum walked in from the hallway carrying some letters. 'Postman's early this morning,' she said, flicking through the envelopes. 'There's something here for you, Josh.' She held up a brown envelope. 'It looks important.'

Mr Palmer was standing at the sink. He turned to Josh. 'What have you been up to?'

Mrs Palmer passed Josh the envelope. Jess nestled up to him and looked over his shoulder as he opened it. His parents watched in silence.

'It's from the Military Services Department,' Josh said with a slight tremor in his voice. 'Something about 'con...con...scription'...whatever that means?'

He cast a nervous glance towards his sister.

She looked back at him with big eyes. 'It's like when they call you up...to fight in the war,' Jess said, looking very thoughtful.

Mr Palmer walked over and took the official-looking

document from Josh. 'It's obviously some kind of joke.' He studied it carefully. 'Mmmm. It's your name all right. Joshua Palmer. DOB's correct. Called up to service on 15th October, 2019...'

'That's today,' Mrs Palmer interrupted, standing by her husband's side.

'...To Aldershot Barracks,' Mr Palmer continued. 'Full medical and three days training.' He placed the document back down on the table. 'Like I said, some kind of joke.'

Now it was Mrs Palmer's turn to pick up the document and study it closely. 'But it looks so real. Someone's gone to an awful lot of trouble.'

Josh sat in stunned silence. He'd no idea what to say.

Jess came to his rescue: 'It's not a joke. It's to do with our Great War theme at school. *They've* sent it. I bet they've sent them out to all the boys in Year 6.' She looked hard into Josh's eyes. 'Didn't Mr Schofield say something about it?'

Josh stared back at Jess and nodded. 'Yes. I remember now. He said something about the boys finding out what it was like to get called up to serve in the war. Nobody knew what he was on about.'

'Well, you know now!' Mrs Palmer said in a more relaxed tone of voice. 'I almost believed it.'

Mr Palmer laughed. 'For Heaven's sake, Alice, he's eleven years old!'

She smiled and handed the paper back to Josh. 'Here... take it back to school. I'm sure your teacher might want to put it in the display.'

Josh took the document from her, put it back in the envelope, folded it and stuffed it in his trouser pocket.

Phew!

No way did he or Jess want their parents to know about the mysterious goings-on, and he was sure they wouldn't believe any of it anyway. He quickly finished his breakfast, got his belongings together and was soon in the car and on his way to school. His mind raced again.

Today *was* definitely the day...and the amazing letter had already kicked things off. He looked in the rear mirror and saw Jess staring at him with a serious look on her face. She looked worried.

'OK, guys...we're here,' Mrs Palmer said as she eased the car through the school gates. 'Have a good day!'

Josh climbed out and looked straight over to the dying poppies. *No sign of the ghostly soldier.* But he still felt tense.

As soon as Mrs Palmer drove out of the school gates and disappeared into the distance, Jess turned to her brother. 'OMG! Who do you think really sent those calling-up papers?'

Josh shook his head and took the crumpled envelope from his pocket. 'I know it sounds crazy...but I think they're real. Remember what Great-Great-Grandad Stanley said...that I'd be *called up* to the *real* Front Line 1.'

Jess put an arm around her brother's shoulder as they walked towards the school entrance. 'It's *not* crazy, Bro. But only you or I would believe it. Just stay calm...go with the flow...and like I keep telling you, I'll be there if you need me.'

Josh nodded and swallowed hard as the two of them made their way to Viking Class.

JOSH GOES TO WAR

The school day started normally enough.

Whole-school assembly went well. Miss Robinson gave out some notices and a few literacy awards for pupils in Year 3, and much to Josh's relief, the Great War theme was never even mentioned. All completely normal!

Lesson 1, English with Mrs Musson, followed by Lesson 2, Maths with Mr Sylvester...both went well, and again, completely normal.

Several times Josh glanced out of the classroom window over towards the poppies...*nothing!*

During Lesson 3, History with Mr Schofield, Josh felt sure 'things' would start to happen. He fidgeted nervously in his seat...but Mr Schofield simply chatted on about the Victorian period and made no reference to the Great War, or anything to do with it.

Josh relaxed a little...until he got an uncontrollable urge to go to the toilet. He fidgeted in his seat and crossed his legs...*but he needed to go!*

'Are you OK, Josh?' Mr Schofield asked him. 'You look tense.'

Josh cast a glance over to Jess. She frowned back at him.

'I need the loo, Sir.'

Mr Schofield nodded. 'No problem. Off you go.'

As Josh left the room, he glanced over at Jess again. She looked back at him with real concern in her eyes!

A moment later he was making his way quietly down the corridor, half-hoping to see a teacher or some pupils maybe...but there was no one. All was quiet.

'Is that you, Palmer?' a voice called out loudly from somewhere ahead of him.

His heart almost ceased beating as the smell of pipe tobacco reached his nostrils. He stopped dead in his tracks...thought about turning...running back to the safety and security of Viking Class. The toilet didn't seem important anymore!

'Don't be afraid, lad. Come on in. I won't bite.'

Against all his instincts, Josh walked on. He reached the room on his left...where the officer had spoken to him previously... and poked his head around the corner.

'Ah! At last! Don't just stand there, lad. Come in and sit down.'

Josh's eyes almost popped out of his head.

Just as had happened before, the room was now an office, with the same man dressed in full military uniform sitting behind a desk covered in papers.

The soldier rose to his feet and saluted. 'Good to see you again, Palmer.'

Josh hesitated, stood to attention and saluted back. As the officer sat down, Josh did the same.

The officer picked up a lit pipe from his desk and drew on it. Josh watched nervously as the soldier puffed out several smoke rings.

'Well, Palmer, as promised during our last meeting, I recommended you for corporal and you've been accepted. Congratulations, Corporal Palmer.'

For some strange reason Josh felt proud – though he knew inwardly he'd no right to.

'You may also remember, *Corporal* Palmer, that I promised you action in Northern France.'

'Yes, Sir!' Josh replied, beginning to wonder if this was all a dream or not.

'Well, we're soon to place your regiment on the Western Front in the Somme area, Palmer. Guaranteed action!'

Josh swallowed hard. Dream or no dream...it seemed lots of things were starting to come together. He took a deep breath and asked the question, 'When, Sir?'

The officer smiled. 'Keen for action, eh, Corporal Palmer? Soon.'

Josh took a deep breath again. 'How soon, Sir?'

The officer stood up, placed his hands on the desk, leaned over and looked Josh squarely in the eyes, 'Sooner than you would ever know, Corporal Palmer.'

Josh wondered what to say next when a familiar voice sounded from behind:

'Josh! What are you doing in here and why are you

talking to yourself?'

Josh swivelled round and saw the Head Teacher with a surprised look on her face. Turning back, he saw that the officer had disappeared. In fact almost everything that had been in the room had disappeared! Glancing around, he saw that he was now in a different room altogether.

'Only teachers are allowed in the stationary store, Josh,' Miss Robinson said to him kindly.

'Sorry, Miss,' Josh said, thinking on his feet. 'I was on my way back from the toilet and I needed a new ruler and I thought I'd see if I could see one...'

'No problem, Josh,' the Head Teacher interrupted. 'Just ask your form tutor. He'll sort out a new ruler for you. Like I said, this room is for staff only.'

Josh apologised again and made his way quickly back to his lesson. With all manner of thoughts swirling through his head, he opened the classroom door, desperate to get back to reality.

He looked straight to Jess. She was writing avidly and never even looked up.

Odd!

He glanced around at the other pupils. *Everyone* was writing or looking down at their desks. No one even bothered to look up at him.

Only Mr Schofield stopped what he was doing and stared across at him. 'Ah, Josh. Good to have you back.'

Josh stared in horror at the teacher's face. Once more, his form tutor had that strange look in his eyes...even more so than before. *A real zombie stare!*

'Don't sit down, Josh. You're wanted!' Mr Schofield said calmly.

The whole class seemed in a trance. Nobody, not even Jess, looked up as the form tutor pointed out of the window.

With his heart beating rapidly, Josh walked over and looked to where Mr Schofield was pointing.

...And there in the dying poppies stood the ghostly soldier, waving a hand and beckoning Josh to join him.

BATTLE FRONT

Almost in a trance himself, Josh left the classroom, made his way out of school and headed over to the poppies. No one stopped him, no one challenged him; the car park between the main school building and the poppies was completely deserted.

...But the ghostly soldier remained, still beckoning Josh to join him, his outline becoming clearer with each and every one of Josh's approaching steps.

As Josh joined the lone figure among the poppies, a swirling mist enveloped them, blotting everything else out completely.

'Great-Great-Grandad Stanley?' Josh asked.

The soldier tightened his rifle strap around his shoulder. 'Aye, lad. That'll be me. And you'll be young Josh...my great-great-grandson?'

Josh nodded.

The soldier looked down at him. 'I'm guessing you got your call-up papers?'

Josh had forgotten all about them. He rummaged in his trouser pockets and withdrew a crumpled brown envelope. 'Got them this morning. Did you send them?'

The soldier nodded. 'Good to get you in the right frame of mind. I remember when I got mine. They put the fear of God in me...and my family. Now brace yourself. We're going places.'

Josh felt surprisingly calm. 'Where exactly?'

'To the front line, lad. Where else? You've been called up.' The soldier removed his rifle from around his shoulder, stooped forward and held it upright on the ground. 'Get hold of it, Josh. Hold on to the barrel. And hold it tight, mind!'

Josh did as he was told. He grabbed hold of the gun. It felt ice-cold.

The soldier knelt beside him, one of his big hands gripping the gun just above Josh's. 'Well then, lad. The time's arrived. Welcome to the *real* Front Line 1.'

As Josh tensed, wondering what was going to happen next, the swirling mist thinned and an acrid burning smell filled his nostrils. From somewhere very close came the sound of gunfire. Blasts from loud explosions all around resounded in his ears.

As the mist cleared completely, Josh found to his horror that he was kneeling in a deep ditch. He knew at once that he was inside a war trench. The ghostly image of Great-Great-Grandad Stanley had vanished.

'OK, Palmer,' a voice boomed from beside him. 'We're

up and over in exactly five minutes. Good luck.'

Josh looked to his left and recognised the officer whom he'd met in school. But this time the officer's uniform was soiled – splattered in mud and torn in several places. The man had a nasty cut on his forehead and blood trickled down his face.

Josh began to panic. He felt very different. He stared at his man-size hands and looked down to his feet and saw that he was wearing big muddy boots. He scanned his body and saw that he was wearing uniform...full-size uniform! Finally the awful realisation dawned upon him.

...He had somehow become the ghostly soldier who had brought him here...Great- Great-Grandad Stanley!

Josh's heart raced like never before. He looked along the trench – first to his left and then to his right. There were other soldiers like himself, peering up towards the top of the trench, their faces filled with terror.

A young soldier had his hands clasped in prayer and was muttering the Lord's Prayer, loud enough for Josh to hear.

'ONE MINUTE, LADS, AND THEN THE WHISTLE BLOWS.'

Josh's heart beat so fast he thought it would explode. He looked down at his big rough hands...they were shaking. He closed his eyes tight shut...wished he could wake up...prayed that this was all some horrible dream.

But the stench of burning and the explosions sounding around him told him that this was real.

A tap on his heel caused him to swivel around. A soldier lay behind him, his shoulders propped up on the back of the trench. He had a blood-stained bandage around

131

his head and his right hand was missing...a bloodied, bandaged stump where it should have been.

'Good...good...luck, Corporal,' the man said with difficulty. 'I...I...hope you make it.' The wounded soldier coughed and spluttered and his body slumped forward.

'FIVE, FOUR, THREE, TWO, ONE.'

PHEEEP!

As the commanding officer blew his whistle the soldiers followed his example and ascended the crude wooden ladders leant up against the trench wall. Josh did the same.

As they emerged from the top of the trench Josh took in the awful sight in front of him.

Swirling smoke enveloped everything, painting the landscape a dirty grey and obscuring the sky. The ground was a mud bath, stretching out into no-man's land, bare and barren, broken only by random skeletal trees, their blackened branches clawing at the acrid air with long-dead fingers.

'CHARGE...'

Josh followed the commanding officer, aiming his rifle directly in front of him. The officer waved his pistol and rallied his men. The adrenalin coursed through Josh's body, making him feel brave and scared at the same time.

CRACK, CRACK, CRACK...

Bullets winged past him from gunfire somewhere ahead.

The commanding officer stopped dead in his tracks, removed his backpack and took two grenades from it. He passed one to Josh and one to a soldier by Josh's side. 'MACHINE GUN TO THE RIGHT...PALMER...

TAKE HIM OUT! OK, MEN...BACK TO IT.'

They charged on again, Josh veering to the right towards the gunfire. The other soldier carrying a grenade stayed close by his side. Josh saw the terror in his young face. He looked no more than a school boy.

Up ahead, the mist and smoke cleared enough for Josh to see the German machine-gunner on top of the enemy trench, the lethal gun mounted on a tripod and firing towards them.

CRACK, CRACK, CRACK...

The young soldier by Josh's side screamed and fell to the ground. He rolled over and stared up at Josh with sightless eyes.

For the first time Josh felt the anger well up inside him. He ran on, swerving from side to side, desperate to dodge the deadly enemy machine-gun fire.

CRACK, CRACK, CRACK...

Josh saw the enemy gunner clearly – no more than a hundred metres away. He pulled the pin from the grenade and prepared to throw it.

CRACK, CRACK, CRACK...

PING!

A bullet struck his helmet but made no impact. *Thank God he was wearing it!*

Josh did what he'd done so many times in his Front Line 1 computer game. He hurled the grenade towards the enemy gunner.

He watched in awe as the grenade sailed over the gunner's head and dropped into the trench behind him.

BOOM!

A combination of intense light and fire erupted from

the trench, the blast killing the gunner instantly and hurling his lifeless body into the air.

Josh felt sick and horrified at what he'd just done. *This was no computer game!*

A familiar voice from over on his left brought him back to his senses.

'WELL DONE, PALMER. ONWARDS, MEN. TAKE THE TRENCH.'

Josh sprang back into action...charging forward with the other men as if his life depended on it...realising with every step that *his life did depend on it!*

He'd wanted for so long to find out what lay ahead of the enemy trench...and now it seemed he was about to find out...*for real!*

THE FINAL TRUTH

Josh approached the enemy trench. He stepped over the enemy gunner's lifeless body and avoided looking down at it. It was more than his heart could take. He took off his backpack, removed the gas mask and prepared to put it on...just like in Front Line 1...but there was no gas attack!

Thank God!

Instead he peered down into the German trench, wondering what he would see. Surprisingly...*it looked familiar.*

The first things Josh saw were the dead bodies, clothed in German uniform, littering the bottom of the trench and surrounded by discarded equipment. It was easy to see that the trench had been home to them for some considerable time.

Just as in their own trench, makeshift shelving contained metal mugs, cans and bottles. Josh descended the ladder into the trench and saw the rough piece of wood panelling leaning against the mud wall with a cracked mirror at head height. Below the mirror was a shelf leaning at 45 degrees, its contents scattered in the mud beneath it...mugs, razors, hair brushes and other familiar everyday items.

Why did it look so familiar?

The sight of the soldiers' day-to-day equipment brought a lump to Josh's throat...the Germans *were* the enemy, but they *were* also human...just like everyone else!

'PALMER...GET UP HERE. THE ADVANCE IS STILL GOING ON!'

Josh quickly ascended the ladder and readied himself to join the continuing charge. Now, finally, he would find out what lay beyond the enemy trenches.

As the Commanding Officer once again blew his whistle and rallied his men to charge forward, Josh stopped dead in his tracks.

No wonder the German trench seemed so familiar. It's like in my dream. Everything's exactly the same!

'PALMER...ONWARDS!' the CO boomed from somewhere in front of him.

But Josh knew exactly what was going to happen next. Sure enough, a sound reached his ears from the bottom of the enemy trench.

'MIR HELFEN! MIR HELFEN!'

Without hesitation, Josh turned and headed back towards the German trench.

'PALMER...GET BACK HERE!' the CO bellowed

from ahead.

Josh ignored the CO's command. A man's life was at stake...enemy or no enemy. He approached the trench wall and peered over. Sure enough, one of the 'dead bodies' was still alive.

Just as in his previous dream, a German soldier lay in the bottom of the trench, crying pitifully, his right leg missing below the knee, a pool of blood growing bigger around him. But this time there was more horror...*rats!* At least a dozen squealing rats scurried across the bottom of the trench, homing in on anything they could feast on. Several rats were feeding on a dead cat over in one corner, others feasting on the corpse of a dead soldier.

'KÖNNEN SIE MIR HELFEN?'

Josh descended the ladder, approached the badly-wounded soldier and handed him his water bottle. As the German sipped gratefully, Josh knew what he had to do. He tore a strip of material from the soldier's ragged trousers and wrapped it tightly around his right thigh.

Josh couldn't believe what he was doing, least of all how he knew what to do. He sensed that Great-Great-Grandad Stanley was still somehow with him.

He took the water bottle from the soldier, picked up a fragment of wood from the trench bottom and handed it to him. The German understood and nodded. He placed the piece of wood in his mouth and bit hard.

Josh brought the two ends of the rag together around the German's thigh and twisted them into a knot... tighter...tighter...tighter!

The German bit hard onto the wood to stifle his agonising pain.

With the blood flow stemmed, Josh tied the makeshift tourniquet...job done!

The German had lost a lot of blood and drifted in and out of consciousness. He looked pleadingly at Josh, muttered something in German and unclasped his left hand. Josh saw the small, crumpled photograph. He took it and looked at it...a young man, a young woman and a baby.

Josh gulped as he realised it was a picture of the German soldier with his wife and child. On the back of the picture something was written in German...the man's name maybe.

Josh clasped his own hand around it and the German smiled...and passed out.

CRACK!

Josh felt something rip into his back followed by the most agonising pain he'd ever felt in his life...*and all went black*.

*

Drifting in the blackness, Josh knew exactly what had happened. He'd been shot in the back by the commanding officer. Proof of what had really happened to Great-Great-Grandad Stanley.

Great-Great-Grandad Stanley was no deserter – and definitely no coward! He'd simply tried to save the life of another human being...enemy or no enemy.

Drifting on through the blackness, Josh wondered if he was really dead. Strangely, he felt no fear – just an overwhelming sense of peace – the nightmare battlefield stuff gone forever! He wondered if those countless dead victims of the Great War had felt the same way.

'But you're not dead, young Josh,' a soothing voice reassured him.

As the blackness faded, Josh looked up from the dim light of the trench bottom and saw Great-Great-Grandad Stanley standing at the top of the trench. He looked spectral...shimmering...like the apparition Josh had first seen standing in the poppies. And he was standing by the side of the Commanding Officer. But the CO looked real. He was still holding his service revolver, pointing it down into the bottom of the trench.

'Come up here, Josh,' Great-Great-Grandad Stanley instructed him.

Josh's mind swirled yet again with confusion. He looked down and saw Great- Great-Grandad Stanley's dead body slumped over the German soldier he'd just saved.

But...but...

He scanned his own body. He was his normal self again. Josh...eleven years old...wearing school uniform.

'Come up here, Josh. No one can see you. Just as they can't see me.'

Josh ascended the ladder to the top of the trench. 'Is that because we're not real?' he asked.

'We're real...but only in the spiritual sense,' his great-great-grandad informed him. 'Unlike *him*!' he pointed to the CO standing beside him...and then down to the figures in the bottom of the trench. 'Or them...they are long gone. Just images of time past.'

Josh stood beside his Great-Great-Grandad as the

CO waved his pistol and ranted on. 'I'LL HAVE NO DESERTERS IN MY REGIMENT, PALMER. THE ONLY COWARD IS A DEAD COWARD.'

They watched as he replaced his pistol in its case and stamped off.

'A brave soldier,' Great-Great-Grandad Stanley said with sadness in his voice. '...But a misguided one. Like a lot of officers in the Great War, he lost sight of the true value of human life.'

Josh looked down at Great-Great-Grandad's big boots, the muddied boots that had just been his...just like the big rough hands he found himself staring at. Finally he looked up at the rough unshaven face, grey and tired, half-hidden in shadow beneath the tin helmet scarred with a small dint from the machine-gunner's bullet. And as Great-Great-Grandad Stanley smiled down at him, Josh saw the *true* kindness in the soldier's eyes, and knew in that moment that he was looking straight into the face of a legendary hero.

'Well, young man...I guess you've finally reached Level 4 at last,' Great-Great-Grandad Stanley smiled. 'And I know that you've always wondered what lay beyond the front line.'

Josh nodded solemnly, though he wasn't so sure he wanted to know anymore.

'Take my hand,' his great-great-grandad instructed him.

Josh did as he was told. A moment later, he and Great-Great-Grandad were soaring upwards, high over the battlefield and looking down below. The first thing they saw was the top of the CO's flat-peaked cap as he charged onwards with his surviving men close on his heels. Some of the retreating German soldiers were turning and firing at them...victims on both sides falling dead in their tracks.

Josh felt sick again at the sight of it.

As they soared higher, the soldiers below disappeared from view. Now they were looking down on an empty barren landscape. The once-green fields below were vast areas of mud littered with dead trees, coils of barbed wire and rusted farm equipment. Worst of all, beyond the front line the landscape was deathly silent – no birdsong, no sign of wildlife...the cloying atmosphere of violence, pain and death seeming to obliterate everything.

Josh felt the tears streaming down his cheeks. 'OK...I've seen enough!'

'Don't be too upset. Remember what I told you... that all would be OK in the end.' And saying this, Great-Great-Grandad Stanley let go of Josh's hand.

Josh screamed inwardly as he began to plummet downwards. He tensed and held his breath, descending rapidly into the hellish scene below.

He closed his eyes and braced himself for the impact. 'WHOAAHHH......'

CRASH!

He landed heavily on his back...*but no pain!*

With his eyes still closed, he heard the unbelievably reassuring sound of birdsong. He opened his eyes and gasped at the sight of the deep blue sky and white fluffy clouds high above his head. He rose shakily to his feet and stared in wonder around him.

In every direction a mass of blood-red flowers stretched out to the horizon...countless nodding poppies creating a

141

striking crimson ocean.

A familiar voice sounded in Josh's head. 'There you go, lad. One for every brave soul that gave his life for the good of all.'

Josh lay back down amongst the colourful blooms and wallowed in them. He rolled in them, jumped up and down in them and threw handfuls of petals into the clear blue air so that they cascaded down on him.

This is surely Level 4...Paradise Won.....GAME OVER!

'Josh...are you OK? Why do you keep saying 'game over'?'

Josh blinked his eyes. He rubbed his eyes. He found himself staring straight at Mr Schofield.

The rest of Viking Class giggled...except Jess. Josh saw the usual worried look on her face.

'Sorry, Sir. I was just having a...'

'Junior moment, Sir,' Jess blurted out.

The rest of the class giggled again. Even Mr Schofield had to smile.

'Well, let's have no more daydreaming, Josh. If you wouldn't mind concentrating on the job in hand.'

The rest of the lesson passed as if nothing unusual had happened and Josh began to wonder if he really *had* been daydreaming.

During lunch he sat and told Jess everything. There was so much to tell that he hardly had time to eat.

'I knew all along that Great-Great-Grandad Stanley was no deserter,' Jess said. 'If only we could prove it.'

Josh finally took a mouthful of mashed potato and nearly choked as he tried to reply. 'Maybe we can prove it,' he said proudly.

'What do you mean?' Jess asked, her face full of expectation.

Josh had been eating his meal with left hand only, casually loading his food onto his fork and looking very relaxed. He knew his mother didn't like to see him eating in this way...she referred to it as 'American Style'.

...But Josh had good reason! His right hand had remained tightly clasped beneath the table. He brought it up and unfurled it slowly. ...And revealed to Jess the small crumpled photograph in the palm of his hand.

EPILOGUE

11th November, 2040...10.50 am and the bells of Rossfield Church stayed silent.

Inside the church a big congregation joined in prayer in remembrance of all those who had died for their country in the Great Wars that had claimed their lives.

Josh Palmer stood towards the back of the church by the side of his wife and two five-year-old twins. His sister, Jess, stood in the row in front of him with her husband and daughter. Behind him his parents, Mr and Mrs Palmer stood with Grandad George.

These days, none of the Palmer family *ever* missed a remembrance service.

Since Josh's ghostly encounters, it had taken him and Jess just over five years to clear Great-Great-Grandad Stanley's name.

With the help of their parents, they had traced the family of the German soldier he'd saved during the conflict. They'd even been over to Germany to meet them and found, to their delight, that they'd had a notebook passed down to them in which the German soldier from World War 1 had described how Great-Great-Grandad Stanley had saved his leg...and consequently his life. It turned out that the German soldier had been taken prisoner and had spent the rest of the war in a British Prisoner of War Camp before returning to his family. He had stated quite clearly in his notebook that he owed everything to Great-Great-Grandad Stanley.

The Palmers contacted the War Office who finally accepted the evidence, reversed the Court Martial verdict and re-labelled Great-Great-Grandad Stanley a hero. They'd even awarded a third service medal posthumously.

...But what had made Josh (and Grandad George) proudest of all was that the name, Stanley Oswald Palmer, had been added to the War Memorial in Manchester.

'Your great-great-gran would have been so proud,' Grandad George had blubbed to Josh and Jess the first time he'd seen it.

Josh looked at his watch. It was 11 o'clock.

BONG...BONG...BONG....

Everyone stood in silence as the church clock struck eleven.

BONG!

The traditional two-minute silence followed, during which everyone remembered those who had given their lives so selflessly during the historical conflicts.

Finally, a young man in full military uniform walked up to the altar, turned to face the congregation and placed a bugle to his lips. As the two-minute silence came to an end, he commenced playing The Last Post.

*...And there beside him stood Great-*Great-Grandad *Stanley, he too in full military uniform, wearing his two bravery medals proudly at his breast.*

The spectral figure looked across at Josh and saluted. And Josh saluted back, holding the posthumous medal aloft with his free hand.

Nobody else saw Great-Great-Grandad Stanley, only Josh. But his sister, Jess, turned and smiled at him...and gave him a 'knowing look'.

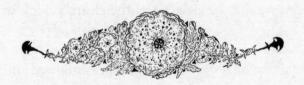

POPPY WARRIOR

ACKNOWLEDGEMENTS

A big 'thank you' to the team for ensuring that this book has been produced to a very professional standard.

To Paul Bryn Davies, the best cover artist ever, to our son, Simon Murray, for his trademark beautiful black and white illustrations, to Millie Deavin for her superb editing, to Lynne and Richard Moore for their thorough proof reading and to Louise Drew for her expertise in typesetting and graphic design. I would also like to thank Ross Bowrage for checking the historical accuracy of this book.

Finally to The Delta Academy Trust for their support - especially to Miss Pippa Robinson, Headteacher of Pheasant Bank Academy, and to her staff and pupils for giving me the inspiration to write this novel.

PJM

Find out more about Peter J Murray's books at:

WWW.PETERJMURRAY.CO.UK